# FELICIA BLACKWOOD

## AND THE REMEDY MYSTERY

DANIELLE RENEE WALLACE

Edited by Nickolas S. Wallace

*To Dad, Mom, Nick, and Ethan, my family:*

*Here we are once again! Thank you, Dad, for being a defender of the truth, an amazing father, and my continual beta reader. I'm always grateful for the time you take with my books as well as for your insight.*

*Mom, thank you for finding the time to read my stories, despite your housewife and mother schedule. I appreciate that you always read them before my publishing deadlines. You're a fantastic mom; thanks for everything!*

*Nick, my trusty editor! First, I'm sorry about the pork rinds. Second, thank you for combing through these books always, even when you've had a long day. You rock. Now, I know you'll even edit this dedication page, so don't add any extra good words in here for you, okay?*

*Ethan, I realize reading stories isn't a main hobby of yours, but I'm thankful to you for being an awesome big bro! Maybe you'll start reading my second book before this third one comes out—or at least after, haha!*

# TABLE OF CONTENTS

# THE SCHOOL AT BEAVER CITY

## Chapter 1

It was the first day of seventh grade, and to be honest, I was nervous. I always did just fine at school—actually, way more than "just fine." I was a straight A student and liked learning, but today was a different first day than before—I was going to a new school. You see, I've lived in Wilsonville, Nebraska my entire life, but I would be going to school in Beaver City, Nebraska, for seventh grade since there wasn't a school in Wilsonville for seventh graders on up.

"Felicia darling, are you nearly ready?"

"Yes, Mother—just finishing my hair," I called to the voice I heard downstairs.

The new school meant the end of a lot of things. The end of sixth grade, the end of walking with my two best friends to school, the end of my mom teaching me full time (she only taught in school full time since January, though, when the school desperately needed a teacher), and the end of my time at the school in Wilsonville. But it was a new beginning, and I was both excited and nervous.

I had always been kind of "weird" because I was rather fond of school and studying and learning all kinds of things. My friends didn't mind, though, and so neither did I.

Once finished braiding a small section of my naturally curly, sandy-brown hair and pulling it up into my high ponytail, I took a quick look into the mirror and thumped down the stairs.

Normally, I put my hair in a ponytail, but the braid was for something a little more special— you know, like the first day of school. The braided section started next to the part in my hair, which then went over to the hairband.

I quickly slipped my feet into my white flats, which were by the end of the staircase, and then I headed to the kitchen.

"Hello, Mother," I said. "I'm ready now. Where's Father?"

My father is named Reece Blackwood, and he is an eye doctor. He didn't have any appointments until later that day, so he was taking me to school in Beaver City.

"He's in his office; he said he needed to check on something, and then he'd be ready."

Before meeting Father, Mother had been Lynette Lothian. She was born in France—Paris, to be exact—but had moved to America at a young age. Therefore, she didn't possess a huge accent. Seeing as her mother was from Paris and her father from New York City, Mother was one-half French and one-half American, making me one-fourth French and three-fourths American. Or something like that.

I went to take my pale-pink, lacy backpack and double checked that everything was in it while I waited. I gave extra goodbye pats to my little white dog, Gracie, who was very grateful.

Father came out of his office with a folder and smiled at Mother. "Goodbye, Lynette."

Then he looked at my little sister, Leanne, who was nearly two, and bid her farewell before heading off.

Coming with Father out the door, I called out a goodbye to my mother and sister.

The drive to the new school was quiet at times,

for I was nervous and got caught up in my own thoughts. But other times I chatted with Father, and then I didn't feel so concerned. Soon, however, we were pulling into the school parking lot, and the nervous feeling came back. I pushed it down, though—my best friends were at this school too, so what was there to worry about, right?

I looked at my father and smiled. "Thanks for the ride!"

"You're welcome, Funnel Cake," he replied, giving me a fatherly hug. "Have a good day. Don't get too worried, okay?"

*He knew I was nervous?*

Exiting the truck, I blushed a little but nodded and thanked him.

Father drove off after I started walking away, and I waved to him as he left.

Walking to the new school building, I wondered if my going to this different place was as hard on him as it was on me. It was a new milestone, after all, and once a milestone happens, you can never have it back; and everything before the milestone goes away as well. Maybe I was being a bit overdramatic on the idea, but who knows?

Anyway, if you were wondering, there was a perfectly good reason for why Father had called me "Funnel Cake" earlier. You see, when I was about, say, six, Father and I had this idea to make funnel cakes together. All his life as a boy, he had helped his mother make them, and he had helped even as a teenager, so therefore he wanted to try the same thing with me. That said, he and I took over the kitchen one day. It was really fun, plus we were doing a rather good job with the cakes; Mother was very impressed. But then, we started goofing off, and I—yes, *I* of all people—rubbed powdered sugar over my face so I'd look as white as a clown. Well, I got the clown look, sure, but ever since then Father had called me Funnel Cake. I suppose I had looked like *that* too.

Now I was nearing the school, and as I got closer, I saw there were kids on my left, on my right, and in front of me, hanging out with their friends and having a good time—which led to an important question: Where were *my* best friends?

"Fay!" two voices shouted in unison.

Well, that answered my question.

I beamed and turned in the direction where the voices had come from.

"Hey!" I chirped, high fiving my friend Kodiak Nobleman (more often than not called Cody) and then giving my other friend, Lydia Arlington, a cheery hug. Having your friends around always made scenarios less intimidating.

"Guess you guys beat me to getting here, hmm?" I asked with a grin.

"We've been waiting for, like, ever, for you to show up!" Cody said.

Lydia playfully rolled her eyes and smiled. "More like five minutes."

"Maybe *you* have," Kodiak playfully replied, "but I'm sure *I've* been waiting for at least fifteen minutes."

"Okay, fine," my friend responded. "Well, Grandmother dropped me off then anyway, and I didn't know you had been waiting so long."

Lydia lived with her grandmother; she had done so ever since her parents died when she was nine.

"Why were you here so early, Cody?" I asked.

"Ryker hit a lot of green lights, so yeah."

Ryker was Cody's older brother by about four years, and he was a junior in high school this year.

"Well, that's nice, anyway," I replied with a smile.

"Speaking of Ryker, where is he anyway?" I asked.

"Hanging out with—oh, that reminds me! You guys should come meet Micah."

Lia (yes, that's Lydia's nickname) laughed.

"Okay, lead the way, then."

And Cody did. He led us carefully through the sea of kids at the school and even kept me from almost tripping over some random, forgotten lunch box. Upon seeing Ryker come into view, he called out a hearty, "Hey, Pitchfork! Over here!"

Cody called Ryker "Pitchfork" because Ryker was thin but strong. It was certainly an amusing nickname, and I wondered what exactly made him pick that of all things as a label for his sibling.

Ryker headed over to us, followed by a boy of about his same size, with light-blond hair and green eyes.

"Hey, Cross Eyes! Hey, girls!" Ryker yelled, grinning. He had the same kind of grin Cody had— the kind that when you saw it, you felt like grinning too.

And yes, "Cross Eyes" was what Ryker in turn called Cody. The thing was, Lia and I had inquired as to why he was called Cross Eyes, but Cody would always just laugh and not answer, and Ryker was no help on the matter either, so it was truly a mystery for me, Lia, and the rest of the world.

Lydia and I greeted Ryker.

"Whoa," he said. "So, who's who today? I can't tell. What's with the matching outfits, girls?"

Lia and I were matching today—deliberately—in cheery, just-below-the-knee-length yellow dresses, light-blue jeans, and white flats. She also had her dark-brown hair in the same style as my hair. It was a fun idea for the first day of school, and Lydia thought it would be funny if people got us mixed up.

We knew Ryker was only joking and that he was well aware of which one of us was which, of course.

"It's the first day of school," I replied as if such a comment was an obvious defense for wearing the same attire, "so naturally we wanted to match."

"If you say so," he replied with a smirk. "Oh, here, let me introduce you to my friend! This is Micah Silvers."

He motioned to the teen with the light-blond hair.

"Cool!" Lia said, giving Micah a handshake. "I'm Lydia Arlington, and I'm in seventh grade—hence the reason I'm here today."

"And I'm Felicia Blackwood," I said. "I'm a seventh grader too."

Micah grinned, said it was nice to meet us, and welcomed us to the new school. He was Ryker's best friend since their freshman year, so I thought it was a little strange we had just now finally met him, but since Micah lived in Beaver City, I guess that cleared things up well enough.

Deep down, I felt a growing excitement replace any nervousness because there were lots of new people here, and I was eager to meet them! With a beam, Lydia gave me a look that said the same thing.

We chatted a bit more with Ryker and Micah, but before long the bell rang, and I readied myself for a day of learning, chatting, and introducing myself.

# Justice and Amity Gravett

## Chapter 2

It was the last class of the day—science—and there were only five minutes left when Miss Lewis, the teacher, started announcing who would partner up with whom for the project she had assigned. I was patiently waiting to find out who I would be paired up with, but Cody's face was white with dread. I was sure it was because he didn't want to get paired up with Trevin Aragon, a very smart but rude boy who had never liked Kodiak.

*Please put me with Lia...* I silently hoped.

The teacher was naming off pairs, and I had very little idea as to who half the kids were. But, of course, I could meet them later. Some kids that had been at the school in Wilsonville now went to the school in Cambridge instead, so I was at this school with only about half of the kids I knew earlier. I hadn't really been friends with any of the kids in school, though—other than Lydia and Cody, of course—so I wasn't too traumatized.

"Okay, and Felicia Blackwood and..."

*Please say Lia.*

"...Trevin Aragon!"

It was as if the whole world came crashing down.

"What!" I yelled, horror-stricken, but then I threw my hand over my mouth and blushed because that was rude. "I'm sorry; pardon me."

That wasn't a good first impression to the other kids—and to the teacher! My face reddened further.

Trevin Aragon sighed in exasperation. Although I couldn't see him, for he was in front of me, I was sure he rolled his eyes. He didn't like me, and I was mostly sure it had to do with the fact I didn't approve of his bullying, and even more so that I was one of Cody's best friends.

Trevin raised his hand.

"Miss Lewis, do I *have* to be paired with Felicia?"

Now it was the teacher's time to sigh. I had heard it was her first year teaching full time, and I was sure she wished the kids would have behaved beautifully.

"Now, look," she said in a sweet voice, "I would like you both to work on this together. You know, I remember becoming best friends with someone I never really liked much until I was assigned a school project with them."

I glanced over at Cody, whose cheeks were now pink, playing around with his pencil awkwardly.

Trevin opened his mouth, likely to retort something, but then hesitated and finally said, "Fine."

The teacher then went on down the list.

"Kodiak Nobleman and Lydia Arlington."

Lydia was sitting next to me, and she leaned over to me a bit and whispered very quietly, "Sorry we couldn't get paired up, but," and then she said even quieter, "imagine how awful it would have been if Cody got paired with Trevin."

For some reason, the comment struck me as funny, and I had to swallow hard so I wouldn't laugh.

Then the bell rang, and everybody rushed— and I mean *rushed*—out of the class as if their life actually depended on it. Well, I didn't hurry so much, and neither did my best friends, or Trevin. But everyone else did.

When Trevin walked past me, he rolled his eyes, and when he got to Cody, he tried to trip him.

"Thanks for class," I told Miss Lewis, whom I was already starting to like very well—even if she did pair me up with Trevin Aragon, of all people. Then, I followed Cody and Lydia, who had already thanked the teacher. They were currently trying to get Cody's locker open, which wasn't working very well.

Lydia was laughing a bit, pounding on the locker. "It won't open!"

"Cody," I asked with a grin, "did you forget the combo?"

"No," he said, "I'm just no good at getting this thing opened. And quite frankly, Lia isn't either."

"Hey!" Lydia retorted, though not truly angry. "I'm trying as hard as I can."

The two tried for another couple of minutes before we heard an older, male voice say, "You need some help?"

We all turned in the direction of the unfamiliar voice, and our eyes fell upon a taller boy. He was in high school, I was sure, and probably about Ryker's age. There was also a girl who looked about his age. They both had dark-brown hair—though the boy's hair was a shade or two darker—and they both had blue eyes.

Cody smiled a little sheepishly. "I guess so. I'm new to this school—seventh grader, from Wilsonville."

"Oh, Wilsonville," the tall boy said. "I've been there before. Anyway, these lockers—some of them are a little odd."

He went up to Cody's locker and pulled the dial out a bit while turning as Cody told him the numbers, careful not to say them so loud that others around us could easily hear. While the boy was turning and pulling out the dial, he also pushed his elbow in part of the door above the dial. Then, the door opened.

"Thanks!" Cody chirped.

The tall boy nodded and held out a hand for Cody to shake.

"I'm Justice Gravett," said the boy.

Then the girl said, "And I'm Amity, his younger sister by a minute and a half."

Lia tilted her head. "You're twins? Cool! My name's Lydia Arlington."

"I'm Kodiak Nobleman," said Cody, "but really, it's fine if you just want to call me Cody. Basically everyone does."

*Justice and Amity are twins…* I thought, and for reasons unknown to either of the new acquaintances, my heart had a longing feeling in it.

"I'm Fay—well, Felicia—Felicia Blackwood."

Amity smiled.

"Felicia? That's a pretty name."

I smiled a bit back. "Thanks. And I like your name too. My mother said *amity* means friendship. I think that sounds like a very peaceful name."

She thanked me and then started talking to Lydia and me about how she thought our matching outfits were so cute.

Justice seemed to be having a nice time talking to Cody, who didn't really have any guy friends, much to his disappointment—except for his older brother, Ryker, of course.

"How old are you both?" Cody asked. "You look like you could be my brother's age."

"Seventeen," Justice replied.

"And juniors now," Amity added.

"Oh, yeah, my brother's a junior, and he's almost seventeen. His birthday's in October, and his name is Ryker."

Amity grinned.

"Oh, Justice," she said, turning to her twin, "wasn't there a boy named Ryker in math today?"

The teen nodded. "Yeah, that's right. I overheard this one kid talking to this other guy and heard that name."

The five of us started heading out the hallway,

making our way outside, while still talking about Kodiak's older sibling until Amity asked how old we were, anyway.

"Thirteen as of the twenty-sixth of July 2004," Cody stated proudly.

"And thirteen as of the twelfth of June 2004," Lydia said with a laugh, referring to her birthday as Kodiak had done.

"*Turning* thirteen on the second of September 2004," I informed the twins, feeling pretty excited that my birthday was so close.

Justice and Amity laughed a bit.

"Well," Justice replied, "we were born on the first of August over here." He motioned to himself and Amity.

When we walked outside, I tilted my face up to the warm sun, knowing I had better enjoy its warmth while I still was able, seeing as the winters could be very long and cold.

Upon looking back down, I saw my father's truck pulling in—though Mother was driving instead because, you know, Father was at work now.

Smiling at my best friends and the twins, I waved and said, "Looks like my mother's here, so I had best be going. It was nice meeting you!"

I hopped into the truck.

After we had pulled out of the school parking

lot, Mom, still concentrating on the road, inquired, "How was school?"

"Good, except for one thing," I said.

"What happened?" Mother replied.

I filled Mom in about the horrors of whom I had been assigned a project with.

Mom didn't reply for a moment as she turned her blinker on and changed to a different lane.

"Well," she said now that we were on the other side of the road, "sometimes those things happen."

She was right, but I sure didn't like it.

Sighing, I responded, "I know. But really, he's the meanest boy I've ever met."

Mom was silent again, thinking. Then she said, "If you think about it, there is nothing you can do other than make the best of the situation."

"How do I do *that,* Mother?" I asked, furrowing my brow. "I mean, he's Trevin Aragon! Plus, I'm sure he's as unhappy about the assignment pair-up as *I* am. Any friend of Kodiak's is an enemy of his, so…"

"Well, regardless of what he thinks of Cody or you or anyone, you're still assigned to work with him. It's just a school project, okay? It'll be fine."

Mother was right, as usual, and so I nodded though I was unhappy.

"And," she said, "I'm pretty sure Trevin could use a dose of kindness, even if he isn't the nicest person you've met."

"What do you mean, exactly?"

"If you think about it logically," Mom began, "you know you have to work with him, and as I said, you had just as well make the best of it. So why don't you invite him over for dinner tomorrow, and then you can work on your project afterward?"

I was silent, unsure how to reply and honestly horrified, because I was sure Trevin Aragon would make horrendous dinner company. He was the last kid on the planet I wanted to invite to dinner.

But I knew telling Mom such wouldn't do any good, and I didn't want to be difficult. Plus, deep down, a feeling inside me said this was probably one of the many times Mom was right on her ideas.

Therefore, I quietly agreed to her plan— though I didn't like it—and dreaded the next day greatly.

\* \* \*

Later, after we got home, I helped Mother in the kitchen. Currently, we were scrubbing sweet potatoes.

"Say, Felicia," Mom began, "who were those two teens with you, Cody, and Lydia earlier today when I came to pick you up?"

I realized I hadn't told her about them yet. How silly of me!

"They're some kids at the school—Justice and Amity Gravett," I said. I then was quiet for a short moment before saying somewhat flatly, a little bit of gloom in my heart, "And they're twins."

I sighed. Genuinely, I thought it was cool and fun they were twins. It was just...

I looked into the sink's water and saw my reflection—a reflection that would have looked just like another girl's.

"Mother?"

"Yes, Felicia dear?"

"Do you ever fear you'll somehow forget her?"

Mother gently sighed and looked at me.

"No. I know I won't ever forget."

And then, with a soft smile, she let out something in between a laugh and a cry, and said, "It's almost like I see her every day—through you."

I never really liked to talk to others outside my family about Sage Blackwood. She was my older sister by three minutes—my twin sister. She had died only two days from birth, and there were times when I longed deeply for a sibling close to my age to spend time with, and a twin would have been... perfect.

But, things don't always go as you wish they would. You can't change the past, but you can choose how to live afterward. And though I knew I'd always long to have had Sage in my life, I knew I was very lucky because I had my sweet little sister, Leanne, and she had done so much good for my family.

Mother smiled softly again.

"And," she said, "I was able to have two days with my child. It may not seem long, but others never get even that much time. It's something others could only wish for."

It was all a matter of perspective, I supposed. I admired Mother for her positive outlook, though I was sure it was difficult.

While scrubbing the sweet potatoes, I looked down at my necklace. I had owned it ever since I was a baby, and Sage was given one just like it too. Mother had intended both of us to wear them when we were old enough, and I had been for quite a while now. The matching necklaces each had a pendant made of pewter in the shape of a heart. On the back of each pendant was an engraving: "The imprint of a sister stays on a heart forever."

Neither of my parents had imagined how hard that phrase would eventually hit us.

But Leanne was my sister, too. When I had found out I would finally get to have another sibling, I... well, I was thrilled and a little bit terrified (for I wasn't sure how to be a big sister, you see). In fact, I cried with joy. Hours were spent getting Leanne's room just right, and I was more than happy to help. After she was born, I got pretty tired with the whole three a.m. crying stuff that happened. But at the same time, I reminded myself that I'd have the cries over the silence any night if it meant I had a sister again.

But the thoughts of my siblings were soon swept away when the doorbell rang.

"Oh, Mother," I said, quickly drying my hands, "I'll get that."

I hurried to the door and opened it only to have my excitement sink.

My eyes beheld an elderly woman by the name of Mrs. Ennis Norton. She was a busybody with a bit of a shrilly voice, who held her head high in arrogance.

"Oh, Mrs. Norton," I said, feeling very disappointed.

"Hello, Felicia," she replied with an air of superiority as she invited herself in, nose high in the air.

I shut the door as she headed toward the kitchen, and all I could hope for was that her visit wouldn't be long.

"Hello Lynette," I heard Mrs. Norton holler in her shrilly voice that got rather high when she yelled.

"I've come to call!"

Maybe Leanne wasn't fond of our company either or it was just some strange coincidence, but she started crying.

I could hear Mother let out a bit of a sigh and ask Mrs. Norton how she was.

"I feel just horrible," was the reply.

I walked back into the kitchen. Mother picked up the rather troubled Leanne and got her to quiet down a bit.

"I'm not sure if I should ask what ails or not," my mother told Mrs. Norton, and then blushed a bit.

Mrs. Norton, however, as if she hadn't heard Mom at all, said, "Did you hear the dreadful news?"

"No," Mother replied. "I don't believe I have. I haven't watched any news lately."

"What a horror it is," our company replied earnestly. "And in our very Wilsonville."

I went back to scrubbing the potatoes. Mrs. Norton tended to find things worse than they really were, so I doubted whatever it was would be a very big deal.

"Just imagine!" Mrs. Norton exclaimed shrilly. "There was a break-in at one of the houses in Wilsonville while the family living there was on vacation. They just got back yesterday, and what a horror it was for them."

Such news actually was quite bad and surprising, rather than the usual stuff she informed us about, and I felt sorry for the family that had been robbed.

"Oh no," Mother said, "that *is* bad news. I shall remember to make sure all the doors and windows are locked."

"I should hope so, Lynette," Mrs. Norton replied. "Just to think—in our very Wilsonville!"

"Yes. I hope whoever committed the crime gets caught soon."

"Oh, yes, certainly," was the reply of Mrs. Norton, her nose tilted up high. "You take such news very well, Mrs. Blackwood, especially after the horrors you must have felt after hearing of how your own dear—"

"That was a long time ago," Mom cut in, her voice calm and a bit monotone.

"Why, Lynette! How are you so at ease? Don't little bits of doubt still creep in?"

Mother shook her head. "No, not really. I have confidence. Change does exist."

"I appreciate your devotion, Lynette," Mrs. Norton replied with an air of arrogance again, "but really, don't you think you should keep a close eye out? Sometimes old ways creep back in on people, you know."

I tilted my head, not sure what the two were

talking about now. "Hmm?"

Mrs. Norton looked at me for a second, appearing faintly surprised, and then she turned back to Mother.

"Why, Lynette!" exclaimed the shrilly voiced company. "Don't tell me you've never informed your Felicia about—"

"That's quite enough, Mrs. Norton," Mother coolly replied.

"But, why leave your daughter in ignorance?"

"Mrs. Norton," Mother again said, "that is quite enough. Can I assist you with something?"

Mrs. Norton arose from where she had been sitting and shook her head. "No."

Mother nodded and walked our undesirable company to the door. "All right. Have a nice evening, then."

I followed the two women to the door.

"Yes, thank you," Mrs. Norton said. "But I still think it preposterous that you haven't said anything to—"

Mother gave her a look. "Mrs. Norton."

Mrs. Norton sighed heavily. "All right, very well. Good *day.*"

And then the busybody walked out and shut—or maybe more slammed—the door.

I turned to Mom.

"What was that about, Mother?"

She sighed. "It's something from a long time ago."

I didn't pry, so I changed the subject. "But really, I am surprised there was a robbery here, right in Wilsonville."

This wasn't the first time a crime had been committed here, but I was shocked nonetheless.

Mother and I talked about the robbery a bit and then moved on to other subjects as we finished dinner. However, I couldn't help but wonder what Mrs. Norton and Mother had been talking about earlier.

# Trevin Aragon's Philosophy

## Chapter 3

Much to my disappointment after the final class, I separated myself from my two best friends, who were also hanging out with Ryker, Micah, and Justice and Amity.

I had to invite Trevin over, which required talking to him before he left school, and so time was running out.

I walked to the other side of the building. It felt as if I was isolating myself from my friends even though I knew that wasn't what I was doing.

Trevin was socializing with some of his buddies. From what I could tell, he wasn't really the head of his group; it was some other kid. All of them were smart, yet bullies, and it certainly wasn't *my* idea to *ever* invite one of *those* boys over for dinner. But duty called.

I waited until Trevin excused himself from his circle of friends and walked away from them. When he got pretty close to me, intending to walk past, I quickly stopped him.

He heaved an impatient sigh. "What do you want?"

Now this was the most dreaded part.

"Well, um… uh… My mom wants me to invite you over for dinner… She says we can work on the school project afterward."

He looked at me with a furrowed brow.

*Well, it wasn't my idea, by any means,* I thought.

For a moment, he didn't say anything. Then, he actually struck me funny because he said, "Wait, excuse me, what?"

It was a sort of polite "excuse me," so that was better than it could have gone.

I repeated myself.

Trevin looked a bit uncertain. "I'm not sure. I'd have to ask."

I nodded, but then he said, "Well, actually, I guess I could ask my mom when she comes to pick me up. Mom's supposed to be here any moment. That's why I left my friends."

I replied, "I left *my* friends because I was supposed to look for you."

Trevin smirked, but it wasn't mean like the smirks I was used to seeing from him.

We both waited in silence for Mrs. Aragon to arrive. Currently, I was just hoping my friends wouldn't see me somewhat hanging out with *Trevin* of all people. That would be so awkward and horrifying that I would be unable to speak, perhaps.

Trevin looked at his watch. "Maybe she's hitting all the red lights."

I laughed a little and almost replied about how Cody's brother had the opposite happen yesterday. But I stopped myself just in time, because talking about Kodiak or his family or even Lydia was probably not a good idea.

Just before the silence got too awkward, Trevin said, pointing, "There she is."

A red pickup came into view and drove up toward us about ten feet away.

Trevin went over to the vehicle, opened the passenger door, and started talking to Mrs. Aragon, a couple of times pointing at where I was standing.

Without shutting the passenger door, he then came back and said he was allowed to come. After speaking, he hopped into the truck and was off.

Feeling slightly awkward, I smiled a watery smile and then headed back to the other side of the building.

When I got to the other side, Cody and Lydia

were still around, though Cody was about to leave—
he was literally holding onto the truck handle. From
what I could tell, having just come into the
conversation, my two best friends were deciding on
what time they would work on their own project.
Apparently, it was going to be the next day at four
o'clock.

"Okay, bye Lia!" Cody chirped. "Oh, hi, Fay!
Catch ya later."

I smiled and quickly waved goodbye before he
shut the door, and then I turned to Lydia.

"Good luck on the science project," I said.

"Oh, thanks! The same goes for you, too."

"I was really wishing we'd get paired up."

"Yeah, me too. Maybe next time, though. Do you
remember the one time where we had a group project
and you, Cody, and I all just happened to get
grouped together? That was awesome!"

"That *was* great," I replied. "It was like it was
meant to be."

We only chatted a little while longer before
Lydia's grandmother came driving up in her
convertible.

"Hi Mrs. Adams!" I said. She was Lia's
grandmother on Lydia's mother's side, so that was
why she had a different last name.

"Hello, Felicia," she responded. "Have a good
day!"

I talked to Mrs. Adams briefly before they left
and then waited only a minute until my mother

showed up, and I hurried into *my* vehicle.

"So," Mom began, "is he able to come?"

"Yes."

"Lovely. How was school?"

"Good—like usual," I replied with a grin, because, you know, I was one of those people who liked school very much.

Mother laughed a little. "I'm glad to hear."

"Also, you just missed Lydia's grandmother; she was here a minute ago in her convertible."

I thought the convertible Mrs. Adams owned was very neat, and I found it quite fun indeed.

"I actually saw her on my way here," Mother said. "She sure seemed to be enjoying the ride!"

I laughed aloud at that statement, picturing Mrs. Adams driving with her medium-length, gray hair blowing in the breeze.

We were silent for a while longer, and then I said, "Mother, the news of the break-in spread very quickly, I think. There was talk of it at school today."

"What was said?" she inquired.

"Not much. No one knows who did it, as far as I know."

Mom nodded. "I figured as much."

"I wonder if Uriah is on the case. You know how he is."

"Mm-hmm," she agreed. "Always searching for justice. He's a nice young man."

We chatted some more, and before long, we were

home. After I finished my homework, I went to help Mother cook dinner. She turned on a track of music her mother had listened to in France all the time. It was nice to have something to hear while working.

"Felicia, dear," Mother began, "I also need you to help me bake a loaf of bread for Will and Natasha."

Will Norton was the son of Ennis Norton. Will and his wife, Natasha, lived in Wilsonville.

"Because of the new baby?" I asked.

"Yes, but even more so because I've heard that Owen is very ill."

I sucked in my breath. Owen is Will and Natasha's son, and he was a newborn.

"That's terrible!" I exclaimed. "Did you find out today?"

"Yes, but apparently, they learned of it last week and hadn't informed anyone then, except for Will's mother."

I nodded. "I'll help you bake the bread, of course. I'm sure Natasha doesn't feel very much like cooking."

I noticed on the fridge a small list of things mother had written to bring to the Nortons.

"What's wrong with Owen, exactly?"

"I'm not sure, but it's serious. Natasha said he'd need much medical attention. She was rather distraught, and it's no wonder."

"I hope he'll be all right," I said, deeply moved.

"Me too…"

Will and Natasha had already faced financial hardship—Will had even lost his job just two weeks prior—and doctor bills weren't going to help matters, I was sure.

The situation felt close to my heart because it reminded me of my own sister who had died so young, and I knew the Nortons must have been terribly upset. And even as much of a busybody as Mrs. Ennis Norton was, I felt sorry for her, too, just becoming a grandmother only to discover this deeply troubling news.

* * *

It wasn't long after Father had come home from work that Trevin Aragon rang the doorbell.

Opening the door as Mother had requested me to do, I said hello to the boy in front of me and invited him in, feeling awkward because this was Trevin, after all.

"Hi…" he said, entering.

"Hello," I replied. "Come in, please."

Trevin seemed very astonished with our house, for he looked all around, even staring at the crystal chandeliers. I will admit that my house was just as fancy on the inside as it was on the outside. It had things like beautiful sofas; pretty rugs; lovely, wooden bookcases (all of which were filled with books); and a piano—not to mention the big, fancy fireplace. I will say, though, that the bookcases had been my grandmother's on my mother's side—as well as the piano—and that the sofas had been on clearance.

Trevin had brought some things for the project and asked where to put them.

"Anywhere is fine, really," I replied. "My mother is in the kitchen, and my father just got home from work."

I headed toward the kitchen, Trevin following behind. He had taken his shoes off immediately upon entering—well, actually, he removed them after he recovered from his shock of the chandeliers. To be honest, though, I didn't mind if he kept his shoes on or not, and I was sure Father and Mother didn't either. However, it was polite, a word I never thought I'd use to describe Trevin.

When we entered into the kitchen, Mom turned around and smiled.

"Oh, you must be Trevin Aragon. I'm Lynette Blackwood."

Trevin responded courteously, a bit of a contrast from the usual Trevin Aragon.

Mother motioned to my very little sister. "And this is my other daughter, Leanne."

Trevin, much to my surprise, gave a halfway smile, and said, "She's cute."

Not much later, Trevin met my father, and we had dinner. I will not go into the details of it other than to say I think Trevin was rather amazed with the double doors that brought us into the dining room; I shall also mention the fact that both of my parents tried to make conversation with him, and he answered all of their questions and gave some in return. Very surprisingly, I found out that I actually felt a bit at ease around the boy because Trevin seemed to feel awkward, too—maybe even as awkward as I felt.

After dinner was over, the table was cleared so the project could be worked on. It wasn't an awfully hard project, and so we finished in a little less than an hour. We were just looking over our work.

"And… done," Trevin said, after he was finished checking. "Easy."

I finished scanning over everything a couple of minutes after him. "It's good to not have to worry about the project anymore."

"True," he agreed. "It wasn't that hard, though. You're pretty smart."

"Oh, thanks," I said. Complimented by Cody's bully? That was… weird.

"Maybe they should pair us up more often," he said.

*I can't say I agree.*

I turned to the bully. "There's a lot of smart kids at school—you hang out with most of them."

"Yeah, sure."

We then started talking about other things. We had only been acquaintances before because, you know, he was Trevin Aragon—a bully.

Therefore, because we knew so little about one another, we began asking questions about things you may tend to find out upon recently meeting someone.

"Do you have any siblings?" I asked. I honestly had no idea and was a little surprised that I knew so little about him.

"Five."

"You're kidding!" I exclaimed, surprised. I had assumed he was most likely an only child. After all, I hadn't recalled meeting any other Aragon kids.

"Yeah, I'm second to the oldest, too."

"How does your dad provide for so many family members?" I asked with a bit of a laugh, my eyebrows up.

"Well, we live in a… rather modest house, so to speak. His job could be better, but he likes it, so yeah."

Trevin looked away, as if he were embarrassed—especially with my house being so fancy.

"Oh," I replied. "Well, I guess it's not really the house that matters—it's who's inside it."

Trevin smiled a half smile.

"You sound like my mother. But my brother helps with the funds some through his job," he explained. "And I'm going to, too, when I'm fifteen or sixteen."

"Really? Where does your brother work?"

"Oh, just at the general store, you know. I'm sure you've seen him before."

I did recall seeing a teenaged boy working there before but never thought much of it until then.

"How old are your siblings?" I asked.

"My older brother, Joshua, is sixteen; my

younger brother, Joel, is eleven; Emilia is ten; Mercy is eight; and Ivy is seven."

"Three boys and then three girls," I said, thinking to myself somewhat. "You've got a pretty big family!"

Trevin half-shrugged. "Yeah, well, it keeps me busy, especially when I need to get my homework done on the weekends."

I laughed a little bit. "I usually do homework with my friends on Saturdays."

I guess I shouldn't have really said that, because as soon as I finished the sentence, Trevin's eyes got all cold and icy like.

"I don't like to associate with those who won't work hard at knowledge."

*That's kind of a weird thing to say.*

"My friends and I do study hard, though..." I said, somewhat confused by the boy.

"Kodiak doesn't."

"He tries very hard at school!" I exclaimed, wanting to defend my friend and also knowing that most kids considered him a dunce.

"The grades don't say so."

That annoyed me.

Although I'm normally soft-spoken, I did have a bit of a temper problem at times. Because of this, I took a deep breath, trying to keep my cool in this situation.

"Just because someone can't manage all A's all the time, doesn't mean they aren't trying hard," I replied, slightly monotone.

"Maybe," he retorted, sticking his nose up into the air a bit. "However, *I* for one am not sure."

"I *know* he is!"

"Hmph."

Trevin had actually been acting pretty nice up until now.

I didn't say anything, and for a while Trevin didn't either. Then he said, "I don't like to see potential go to waste."

"What? What do you mean?" I inquired.

"If one spends all their time helping another get good at studies, then the one helping can't excel as far as they could."

Furrowing my brow, I replied, "I'm not sure I'm following."

Trevin rolled his eyes. "Really, Felicia. There's no question about it that you've got talent. The problem is that you help Kodiak with his homework on weekends when you could be studying even deeper."

"Isn't helping others supposed to be a good thing?" I said. "We've all got to start somewhere."

Trevin pointed his nose up into the air again. "You have much potential, yet you refuse to cultivate it."

"That's not true," I responded. "I study on my own time too. But I think it's fun to work on stuff with my friends. We all work together to learn, and if I can spend some of my time helping with that, then it's only a good thing."

"I agree with you on working with others—yet, not on *who* the others should be," Trevin Aragon arrogantly said. "I should think working with those who are as passionate about study as you are should be a top priority."

*Trevin's ideas are a bit strange.*

"To be honest," I began, my heart sighing a bit, "I can't say I'm with you on that."

Trevin sighed in exasperation as he rose from his seat, slammed his book, and gathered up his things. "That's disappointing, really. You have a lot of potential, like I said, but I'm afraid it'll have to go to waste."

His nose went up into the air again as he stiffly thanked me for inviting him over, and then he thanked my mother, though not so stiffly, before taking his leave.

\* \* \*

"Thanks for helping me get stuff ready for the Nortons."

"You're welcome, Mother. I was happy to help."

Mom and I were currently walking up Will and Natasha's driveway to bring the things over. I was carrying Leanne, who didn't always like walking on her own. Mother had talked to Natasha on the phone, and Natasha said she was home, so it would be fine to come over.

The Nortons' house was old but beautiful. The outside walls were brick; the shingles on the roof were a dark-red kind of burgundy; and the driveway was clean, with not even a twig or leaf on it. Will's father had sturdily built the house himself, plus Natasha was a hardworking and devoted housewife. Therefore, their home was wonderful inside and out, even if the building was on the older side.

When Mother and I got to the door, Mother knocked, rather than ringed the doorbell, because she said the bell might wake up baby Owen if he was asleep.

The door opened a minute later, and Natasha stood in the doorway.

"Hi ladies," she said with her usual sweet smile. "Come in."

Mother and I walked into the cheery house after greeting Natasha, and we followed her into the living room. I enjoyed the cozy feeling of the place, with its soft, thick carpet; lit candles on the fireplace mantle and coffee tables; and lots of sweet pictures. Honestly, the inside of the Nortons' house reminded me of Lydia and her Grandmother's house, just that it was bigger than Lia's and that the outside looked quite different.

I lowered Leanne back to the ground.

Natasha Norton was a pretty woman in her early thirties with wavy, auburn hair; sea-green eyes; and a smile that could brighten anyone's day.

"Here, Tasha," Mother said, giving Natasha the things we brought. "How've you been?"

"Thank you so much! Things are going

wonderfully now that you girls are here for a visit. Here, have a seat and make yourselves at home."

Owen was in a little bassinet, sleeping peacefully in the living room. I noticed he looked rather pale and that he was on the smaller side.

*Poor child,* I thought to myself, my heart breaking.

Natasha set down the items on the counter and thanked Mother again, then took a seat next to Owen's bassinet. Mother and I sat down on a couple of fancy velvet chairs.

"So, what's been up with you ladies?"

"Well," Mother began with a smile, "Felicia here just started seventh grade."

"Oh, did you?" Natasha asked. "I remember those days. Seventh grade was fun."

"I like school a lot," I said with a grin. "But I had to go to Beaver City this year since the school here in Wilsonville only goes up to sixth grade."

"Oh, Beaver City! That's where Will went to school. I went to the school in Cambridge though."

"Really?"

Natasha and I talked a bit about the two schools, and then she, Mother, and I switched gears to other matters.

"Lately I've just been keeping busy," Natasha said, "from taking care of a newborn, to housework, to doctor appointments, to Will losing his job…"

"I'm terribly sorry," Mother said softly. "Do let us know if you need anything."

"Oh, I will, Lynette, thank you." But then she beamed greatly and somewhat whispered to us, the tone of her voice obviously excited, "Will's finding out tonight if he's getting another job!"

"Oh, that's wonderful!" Mom exclaimed, and I agreed.

"It'll be here in Wilsonville, right?" I asked.

"Mm-hmm!"

"That's great!"

If Will could get the job, Owen would be *sure* to get better because he could get the medicine he needed.

*And then everything will be all right.*

If only that had been what actually happened.

* * *

I had never been so relieved to be done with a school project than when Trevin and I had finished ours. I could conveniently go back to spending time with my best friends, helping Cody with math, and having sleepovers with Lydia. And there was always that wonderful thirteenth birthday party coming up to look forward to.

Anyway, there is this old bus my friends and I like to go in. It's kind of strange because it's abandoned in an alley and for some reason is crammed full with books. I wasn't sure why it was there, exactly. It had been stolen by robbers years ago, and Lydia's mother had found it when she was a girl. Lia had rediscovered it, and it had become one of our usual hangout places.

Anyway, we were headed there, the three of us—Cody, and Lydia, and I.

"I can hardly wait for your birthday, Fay," Cody said, "because you're having cake, right?"

I laughed. "Yes, of course."

"Well, you can count on me being there, then," Kodiak replied with a smirk.

I turned to Cody and teasingly asked, "Do you think Ryker's coming just for the cake?"

"Yeah, of course!" he replied, pushing his strawberry blond bangs out of his eyes. "Just kidding. He likes hanging out, so I doubt the cake matters. Say, Fay, are you having punch?"

"Yes, but Mother's making it pink."

"Eww!"

"I, for one, love pink," I responded, "very much."

Lydia grinned. "I like pink too, but purple has always been a personal favorite of mine—and navy."

"Well, I like blue best," Cody explained. "I like really any shade of blue, to be honest, but light blue is my most favorite. And I like orange, but peach is ugly."

"Peaches are tasty, though," Lydia said, grinning.

"That's true. But the color's ugly."

The bus came into view, and we quieted for a moment. It mysteriously sat there in the ally, like always, full of ever so many books. How strange it was indeed!

"I should have brought Charity. She loves the

bus!" Lia said, turning to me with a happy look.

Charity is Lydia's dog. She was with Lydia on the day she discovered the bus.

"And I should have brought Gopher," Cody replied. Gopher is one of Cody's dogs. If you're wondering, Cody doesn't have any actual gophers as pets.

I laughed. "And I guess I should have brought Gracie, then."

Opening up the bus door, Lydia peered in.

"So, what are we looking for today," she inquired.

"Anything on horses?" Cody asked. Cody lived on a ranch, and he and his stallion, Nightfall, had participated in rodeos together. He loved reading about horses.

"I did see a horse book in here the other day," Lydia responded. "I'll take a look and see if I can find it."

My friend did her searching in silence, and Cody and I were silent too, waiting patiently.

"Well, I thought I had put it over—ow!"

"It wasn't me this time!" Cody quickly clarified.

"I know…!" Lydia yelled from the inside of the bus. "It's just that this huge book fell—right on my foot."

Cody turned to me and grinned a little bit, his hazel eyes merry with amusement.

Then Lydia shouted, "Here it is! The horse book, that is."

She came out, book in hand, and gave it to Cody to borrow.

"Thanks, Lydia!"

"Yep. Need anything, Fay?"

"I guess I'll take a look around," I replied.

Entering the bus, I breathed in the smell of old books, convinced it was one of the best smells in the world.

I looked around at various books, marveling as to how anyone would ever desire to steal them and stack them all up here. It was such a rude thing to do!

I picked out a couple that had to do with dress-making pointers, seeing as I loved to sew clothes, and then headed out.

Lia laughed. "Up to some more sewing, Fay? I would grab a book or two so I could read about sea creatures or something, but I've already got plenty of them that I'm borrowing at home."

I shut the bus door, and the three of us left the alley.

As we walked, we chatted about various things, including the robbery, about which Kodiak said he was going to ask Uriah.

Lydia pushed a strand of dark-brown hair out of her face. "Everyone seems to be pretty worried."

Cody nodded in agreement. "I heard someone mention it in the store, a couple kids discussing it at school, and even someone talking about it at the doctor's office!"

Lydia laughed a little. "The doctor's office?"

"Yeah, Nightfall accidently stepped on my foot."

"Ouch," Lia said, grimacing. "And I thought having a book fall on my foot was bad! It did look like you were kind of limping today, Code."

"Is your foot okay?" I asked.

"Yeah, thankfully," Cody replied. "Mom got all scared, though. It's bruised up, but I'm definitely glad it isn't broken. I think Nightfall kind of realized my foot was there before he put any more pressure on it than he already had. He's smart like that, you know."

"Well, I'm glad it's okay," Lydia said. "I cringe at the thought of his full weight on your foot."

I heartily agreed, and then, after some further discussion, we fell silent. I remembered that I needed to get back home, so I bid both of my friends goodbye and hurried to my house.

# THE INTERN

## Chapter 4

When I opened up the front door and entered in, Father was already home from work, talking with Mother in the kitchen. I picked up Gracie as she ran to greet me and pet her soft, curly, white fur. Walking into the kitchen, I chirped, "I'm home!" but not too loudly, because Leanne was sleeping in her room, and I didn't want to wake her up.

Dad and Mom greeted me and told me to have a seat.

"Your father has some news," Mother said.

"Okay," I replied, surprised. "What is it, Father?"

Dad finished sipping his coffee and said, "I've

officially got an intern."

"Really?" I asked.

Dad nodded with a smile. "Mm-hmm, Funnel Cake."

"That's so wonderful!" I cheered. "Who is he?"

"His name is Miles Carpenter. He's twenty years old and just moved from Dunning to Cambridge a month ago."

"Neat!" I chirped.

"And," Father began, "his mother came to America from Chile years ago, just like how your mother came from France."

*Chile! How beautiful!*

"Oh, wow," I breathed. "When does he start working for you?"

"Tomorrow. Actually, he'll be over here tonight, though, because I'm going over some stuff with him in my home office."

"That's so great, Father! I'll be looking forward to meeting him."

Mother agreed. "From what I've heard, he seems to be a very nice, polite young man."

I grinned. *An intern?* It was unexpected, that was for sure, but I couldn't wait to meet this respectable person. The more I thought about it, the more excited I became.

\* \* \*

"Hello, ma'am, I'm Miles Carpenter."

Father's intern had just arrived at the house.

"Why hello there!" Mother replied with a smile. "It's nice to meet you. I'm Lynette Blackwood, and this is my daughter, Felicia."

Shaking the intern's hand, I smiled and said, "Hello sir." Miles beamed and greeted me as well.

His hair was a very dark shade of brown—so dark that it was almost black—and he had brown eyes. He appeared to be about a couple of inches below six feet tall and was a little thin.

Father, after shaking hands with his intern, brought Mr. Carpenter to the office.

Following them both, I entered the room too, breathing in the scent of one of Father's candles, labeled "Savory Apple Pie." I knew Father wouldn't mind if I came in with them. Plus, I thought his work was interesting.

They went to Dad's desk and sat down on a couple of nice chairs, Father pulling some papers out of one of the drawers.

"So you see, Miles, this is one of my patient's latest eye exams. Now, as you can see—"

"No pun intended," I interrupted with a laugh.

Father grinned. "As you can see, it shows my patient's date of birth, his address, and his phone number."

"Mm-hmm." Miles was scribbling stuff down on a pad of paper.

"But now, if you look in this column over here, you can see his eye prescription. He is getting contact lenses. So, let me tell you about all these numbers…"

They went right to work, Miles following along quite well. I didn't understand very much, but it was interesting.

"Now, you see, Miles," Father said after they had gone over the prescription, "here is a section for any notes, in which you can see there are a few things listed. And then there is my signature right there at the end."

"Great. Thanks, Mr. Blackwood!"

"No problem. So next, I'm going to show you some things on my laptop."

"Okay."

They set to their work again, Father pulling up this great big picture of an eyeball. I found this part in particular rather fascinating, so I watched carefully.

Father began to talk about things like glaucoma which was this bad thing that usually happened to older people, rather than younger. Miles already knew how people tested for it, but I didn't.

Dad even talked about laser eye surgery, which made me cringe. That sounded painful. If you did it, though, you wouldn't have to wear glasses or contacts, but it was really expensive.

As he briefly explained some things about an infection called conjunctivitis—also known as pink eye—I was impressed by all the many things Father knew.

He asked Miles some questions, all of which were answered correctly, and Father said he was incredibly pleased and glad Miles was getting a good start at an early age.

"Thank you, Mr. Blackwood. I'm really excited to be your intern!"

Father modestly replied that he was pleased and that he was glad to have Miles work with him.

"Anyway," Dad began, "I think that wraps it up for today. You'll start working with me at the office tomorrow."

"I'm looking forward to it! I've always thought all the equipment was neat in eye doctors' offices."

Father laughed a little and grinned. "Good, because there's a lot of it to see."

He put up the papers they had been looking at, turned off his laptop, and then rose. Father, Miles, and I left the office, and I shut the door.

Mr. Carpenter intended to leave very shortly after, but Mother insisted he stay because she was just about to take a cherry pie out of the oven. Father encouraged him to linger a while as well. So he did, thanking them both and shaking hands with Dad while saying he had smelled few things as good as that cherry pie.

* * *

I was a teenager.

It was the second day of September 2004—my birthday. I was really thirteen, a teenager! The doorbell had rung and I went to open it, humming its pretty chime.

Opening the door, I was instantly greeted with a "Happy birthday, Fay!"

It was Cody and Lia.

"Thank you! Come in."

We always celebrated birthdays together, and I wouldn't have had it any other way—especially on my thirteenth birthday. The two came in, followed by Cody's parents and Ryker plus Lia's grandmother. All our families liked to spend time together, and so we were all here. They each greeted me and wished me a happy birthday, which caused me to blush a little.

I smoothed down my "birthday dress" a bit and thanked each of them. I loved to dress up for special occasions, and Mother said a thirteenth birthday was always a special occasion. My dress was pale pink—which wasn't surprising, as it is my most favorite color in the whole world—and the skirt was ruffled. Mother had put my sandy-brown hair down, rather than up in its typical ponytail, with a large, pale-pink bow in the back. My hair was curly, as usual. When

Mrs. Nobleman said I looked very pretty, I blushed even harder than I had been.

"How do you like being a teen?" Ryker asked with a grin, playfully punching my arm after entering my house.

"It's marvelous," I replied. "But not being a teen was also marvelous."

Ryker lightly laughed.

I was just entering into the kitchen, where Mother was chatting with Mrs. Nobleman and Lia's grandmother, Mrs. Adams, when Cody shouted, "Hey Fay, where's the cake?"

I playfully rolled my eyes, and Lydia laughed at Cody, saying, "It sounded like you were in the process of raiding Fay's refrigerator, and you couldn't find the dessert, so you were all like shouting, 'Where's the cake?'"

This caused Cody to snort, and he pretended to raid an imaginary fridge.

Again, I playfully rolled my eyes. "Mother hid it because she knew you'd try to find it," I responded.

Cody's jaw dropped, and he blushed a bit.

"Really?" he asked in total belief and embarrassment.

"Ooh!" Lydia yelled, teasingly. "Somebody got *busted*." She particularly drew out the *-ed* in *busted*.

Looking at Cody, I replied with a laugh, "No, silly! I'm only joking. It's not in the fridge, though."

The blush faded away from Cody's cheeks. "Oh, phew! Well, where did she put it, then?"

"I don't know. Mother doesn't want me to see it because it's a surprise."

Lia beamed. "I wonder if it will have thirteen pink candles."

Kodiak looked as if a lightbulb went off in his mind. "When my grandmother had her birthday, my family and I were in Mississippi—you know, where she and my grandfather live—and I baked a cake for her with my mom, and we tried to put all the candles on the cake, one for each year."

"What happened?" Lydia asked.

"Well, you see," Cody began, "I didn't have enough candles and I had to go to the store, but the cake was full."

"Of candles?" Lydia further inquired.

"Yeah. I guess the cake needed to be one of those big, rectangular ones."

"Um, Cody," I said, "you're kind of implying your grandmother is really old."

"I don't know, it's just hard to fit that many candles on a cake."

Lydia laughed. "When my grandmother has her birthday, we always just stick to the candles that are already numbers. Grandmother says that's better because she wouldn't want to burn the house down."

"Believe me, that's what my grandmother

decided on too," Cody explained.

I was laughing. "Well, I don't think we have to worry about that for *me.*"

"Not this year, anyway, Fay," Cody said. "Probably next year, though."

"Uh, Cody, what does that mean for you?" Lia asked. "And me. We're both going to be fourteen before she is."

Cody realized his comment had just backfired on him. He let out an embarrassed laugh and said, "Okay, you win, Fay."

"Anyway," Lydia began, turning to me, "what did you get for your birthday?"

"Oh, Lia, that's right, I didn't tell you," I replied. "I got the loveliest present. I'll show you."

Lydia followed me up the spiraling staircase, and Cody did too—after a moment of hesitation because, you see, Kodiak most likely figured it would be something girly, so he wasn't as interested as Lia was.

I walked into my pale-pink room, and carefully grabbed the treasure off of my nightstand.

One look at the possession and Lydia beamed. "Oh, Felicia! What a beautiful box."

"I'm ever so fond of it, for as I will show you, it's a *music* box!"

"That's so neat!" Lia chirped. "Grandmother has one that her parents gave her, and I think it's just wonderful."

"Oh yes," I agreed. "I've always loved music boxes, but I've never had one. This was Mother's when she was a girl—back when she lived in France."

Inside the box, you could see the pieces that played the music. The box was painted red, with fancy gold designs to make it complete. It was really quite lovely.

"What does it sound like?" Lydia asked.

I wound it up, and then let it play its lovely music.

Cody playfully rolled his eyes. "Too *girly*."

"Well, what did you expect?" Lia inquired with a laugh. "We're giggling schoolgirls!"

"True."

I set the delightful music box down on the nightstand and let out a little bit of a sigh.

*Today would have been someone else's birthday, too.*

I only let myself dwell on the thought for a moment and then forced my mind elsewhere.

"Oh," I said, "and Father made me these lovely crochet hooks."

Each of the three crochet hooks had fancy little carvings at their handles in addition to the regular curve that forms a hook on the end of them.

Lydia grinned. "That's so cool!"

Smirking, Cody said, "Should've been knitting needles."

"Come on, Cody," I replied. "Everyone knows I can't knit; I can only crochet. *You,* on the other hand, are quite the knitter."

It was true. Kodiak was surprisingly good at knitting, though he was kind of embarrassed about such, while Lia and I had never grasped how to knit. She and I were very much into crocheting, though.

Cody blushed a bit. "Well, thanks." Changing the subject, he then asked, "What's that?"

I turned my head to what he pointed to: a little porcelain thimble with "Felicia Jade" engraved on it in a cursive font—also one of my birthday presents.

"It's a thimble, Cody. You know, for sewing."

"Oh."

Lia laughed a little. "You use it to push the needle through if you're sewing thick material."

"I think my mom has one of those," the strawberry-blond boy replied. He then sighed exaggeratedly in a bit of a joking way and said, "But this is *too* girly. Can we change the subject?"

I pushed a strand of curled hair away from my face, playfully rolled my eyes, and said, "What game shall we play?"

"I vote tag," Kodiak responded quickly.

"I don't know. We can't play it in the house," I replied. "We'd just knock something over."

"We could play it outside."

"Well," Lydia said, joining in the conversation, "you're too fast, Cody. I can't ever tag you."

"I can't either," I agreed.

"I'm not too fast for Ryker," Cody defended.

"He's older and he's your *brother,*" I responded. "He's used to having to chase you all the time."

"Then let's play one of those games where you balance the egg on the spoon and you have to hurry to the finish line before the others."

"If we were at your house, yes, but Father and Mother wouldn't want us to, because if we dropped one, we'd get the backyard cement all dirty. Your parents are already used to you soiling the cement," I joked.

"True. And I'm already used to cleaning it."

"Croquet?" I asked.

"Nobody plays croquet these days. That was back in the Victorian times, Fay, and we're in 2004," Cody said.

"I suppose so," I replied slowly. "But why does that matter?"

"Fay's house is Victorian, anyway," Lydia explained.

Cody shook his head. "If any of the guys at school saw me playing croquet with a couple of giggling schoolgirls, they'd never let me live it down."

"Well, didn't your Mom teach you to macramé?" I asked. "Nobody teases you about that. Or knitting," I encouraged.

"That's only because I don't let them know."

"Knitting or no knitting," Lia began, "we still don't know what to do. Hide-and-seek?"

"We always play hide-and-seek," Cody replied.

"Yeah," I said, "but not at *my* house. That means there will be new hiding spots. We can play anywhere but Leanne's room because she's asleep."

The thought of different hiding spots persuaded Kodiak. But then none of us really wanted to be the one to seek, so Lia volunteered as tribute, saying that Cody could go after her, and then I'd go after him. It was my birthday, so they said I didn't have to seek first since that's never quite as fun—in our opinion, anyway.

As soon as Lia began counting, Cody practically zoomed out of the room and down the stairs. I hurried to the kitchen, where the ladies were socializing; sat down on one of the chairs; and grabbed Father's newspaper, quickly using it to hide myself.

"We're playing hide-and-seek," I whispered to Lia's grandmother, "so don't give me away."

Mrs. Adams smirked and assured me she wouldn't. The look in her eyes seemed to suggest she remembered what it was like to be young.

In the living room, I faintly heard Cody whisper, "I'm hiding behind the couch," and then Ryker laughed a bit.

Soon, I heard Lia coming down the stairs. It then sounded like she turned into the living room.

*Good luck, Cody.*

"Hmm…" Lydia wondered aloud. "Where are they?"

Then from what I could hear, she turned and came into the kitchen.

*She didn't notice him! But now she's here…"*

There really weren't many places to look for someone in the kitchen, so I figured it wouldn't be long till I was doomed. However, she seemed to look under the table and then around the island counter before walking out, leaving me unnoticed—all the while with the other ladies talking at the table!

Lydia searched around for several minutes before I heard her find Cody, and then the two of them entered the kitchen.

"Aha!" Lydia yelled, grabbing the newspaper and pulling it back a bit to reveal me. "Found you."

Cody, having not noticed me, nearly jumped out of his skin.

\* \* \*

While celebrating my birthday, the doorbell rang, and Father got up to answer it.

"Oh, hello, Miles. Come in."

"Hi, Mr. Blackwood," Miles Carpenter said. "I hope I'm not interrupting anything; I saw the trucks parked outside and figured you guys were likely having people over, but since I'd driven here, I figured I'd check just to be sure."

"Oh no, that's okay. It's my Fay's birthday today."

"Ah, well happy birthday, Felicia."

"Thank you, sir," I said respectfully.

"How many years?" he asked.

"Thirteen!"

"That's really exciting." Miles smiled. "Good times."

He then turned to Father. "Sorry to show up unexpectedly. I know we work together on Thursday evenings and thought we were still on for today."

Father looked apologetic. "Oh, I'm so sorry! I forgot to tell you I was canceling today. I can't imagine how I failed to inform you of that."

"It's fine," Miles said and then smiled. "Well, I really won't be long, but while I'm here, I do have a question."

"Sure, what is it?"

"Well you see, Mr. Blackwood, my brother was thinking he might move to this area because of multiple reasons—one being that he would really like to be in the same area with me again."

Father nodded, and Miles continued, "I was just

wondering if you knew of any banks around here that were looking for more employees. As you know, I live in Cambridge, but I was wondering if you knew of any cities in this general area. He works at a bank and doesn't really want to work just anywhere."

"Oh, yes," Father responded. "Hmm... Well, I'm not sure. I would recommend maybe seeing if Beaver City makes the cut."

Miles thanked Father. "I'll be sure to check that out, Mr. Blackwood."

I tilted my head a bit. "You think your brother may move to Beaver City or around here? That's neat. I'm going to Beaver City for seventh grade right now."

Miles nodded. "Mm-hmm. I would really enjoy having his company around."

"Well actually," Mother began, "when I was out earlier this week at the bank here in Wilsonville, I do believe I overheard the banker saying something about needing a helping hand. It's no wonder—ever since that house robbery, people have been a little on edge. I suppose I can't blame them."

"I'll check with the banker today while I'm in town! Wow, thanks, Mrs. Blackwood!"

Miles wished me a happy birthday again, thanked us for our time, and then left, seeming rather enthusiastic as he did so.

# A Message Lost, Found at Last

## Chapter 5

Lydia and I always loved to have sleepovers together, and we *would* have had a sleepover on my birthday, but Lia couldn't come on that day. She and her grandmother had something planned. Therefore, we determined to have the sleepover the night *after* my birthday.

Anyway, Kodiak, Lydia, and I had gotten out of school at Beaver City and had decided we would like to make a trip to the bus. Cody was going to return a couple of books he had borrowed, and Lydia was wanting to find a mystery to read. I wasn't really searching for anything, because I had received a rather interesting novel for my birthday and desired to finish it first. I don't like trying to read too many different things at once!

Upon reaching the bus, Lydia carefully opened the door and put the books Cody handed her back where they belonged.

"I won't be long," she said to us from the school bus steps.

"Oh, it's no trouble; take your time," I said.

Cody was climbing on top of the bus—something he had a tendency to do. "Yeah, it doesn't bother me. I love it here!"

Deciding *I* would like to take a look around, I headed inside after all. I might find something I'd like to read after I finished the novel, so it wouldn't hurt to look while I was here.

"Oh, Lia, look!" I exclaimed, holding up a story excitedly. "A book about a princess and a prince!"

Lydia laughed a bit. "That sounds right up your alley."

"*Boring,*" Cody replied outside from the top of the bus. "You should talk to my mom, Fay. She likes girly stuff like that, but I find it enormously mushy. Bleh. Nasty."

"Well, I like princess stories," I replied.

"Oh of course *you* do. *I'd* rather read about gun-slinging cowboys!"

Cody's voice got particularly excited when he

said the last word, and then he started to ramble about this one novel he read, explaining something about the cowboy going to a secret hideout and, by chance, discovering the plans of some crooks making plans to blow up a goldmine.

We laughed a little at Cody, and then Lydia grinned at me, a different thought having just struck her.

"Say, Felicia," she began, "when was that choir thing you're doing in Cambridge going to be?"

"Oh!" Cody exclaimed, leaving the remainder of the story explanation behind. "My mom can't wait for your choir."

I laughed. You see, I had been in choir for seven years through a group in Cambridge and really enjoyed it. Kodiak's mother had been in choir when she was a girl, so naturally, she liked that I did it too. And surprisingly, Cody's older brother, Ryker, was also in the choir with me; he had been since I was seven and he was eleven. When Cody turned ten, Mrs. Nobleman was hoping—but to no avail—that Cody would join too, but he said he would die of embarrassment with all those eyes looking at him and that his voice was no good anyway. He said he'd rather end up eating dirt from getting bucked off a horse than be required to sing in front of people in a choir. Lydia and I both thought he would've been a good fit, though, had it not been for his discomfort. He sang fine, even if he didn't think so.

"I don't have the event with the choir until the twenty-second of October," I told my friends.

"Right after Pitchfork's birthday!" Cody chirped.

Pitchfork's—I mean, Ryker's—birthday was on the seventeenth of October.

"It's pretty cool that you and Rhys get to be in the choir together," Lydia said with a grin. Rhys was Ryker's occasional nickname. "We should just get me and Cody in it and have a full team."

"No…!" Cody exclaimed from outside. "I could never."

"Well I'm with Lia on the matter," I said. "I would be all for you guys joining."

"I wouldn't," replied the strawberry-blond boy. I supposed there was no helping it; Cody couldn't be persuaded.

Lydia tried to hit some random high note, deliberately making her voice painfully piercing, which made us all laugh.

Sobering up from her joking, she suddenly sighed contently, "This is one of the most wonderful places in the world."

As she said this, she traced her finger down a stack of books. Stopping at an interesting one, she carefully pulled it out and read the back cover.

"This looks like an interesting mystery. It's about a robbery."

"Hopefully not about the robbery that occurred

here in Wilsonville," I replied.

Lydia held the book up to her nose and breathed in. "I love the smell of books."

"As do I," I agreed.

Lydia opened the book up to the title page, and I noticed a surprised look cross her face.

"What is it, Lia?" I inquired.

I heard Cody thump off the bus.

Looking inside the book, I was shocked.

Cody walked in, but then stopped in the entrance. "What's wrong?" he asked upon seeing our faces.

Tucked in between the front cover and the title page was a photo of a man, his wife, and a young child of eight or nine.

I carefully picked up the photo, and Cody, mindful to not knock over any books, joined Lia and me.

The strawberry blond boy gasped. "Hey…!" he exclaimed. "That's… That's Mr. and Mrs. Blackwood!"

"Yes…" I said. "And that's *me.*"

Lydia furrowed her brow and shook her head a bit. "I wonder why it's in here."

"I… I don't know."

Gently turning the photo over, I sucked in my breath. There was a small, delicate paper with little flower prints tucked in between the book pages and picture.

"Handwriting!"

"It's more than that," Lydia said, her brown eyes very wide. "I'd recognize that cursive style *anywhere*. It's *Mother's*."

We all crowded in a bit closer.

I cleared my throat and read the letter aloud:

> *Dearest Lynette,*
>
> *I know it has been awfully hard for you lately, with Reece being so upset. I pray for you and your lovely little family every day. Please let me know if I may help you in any way, sweet friend.*
>
> *Much love,*
> *Liliana*
> *April 6, 2001*

I kept quietly reading the letter, over and over.

"Father had been upset?" I said, somewhat to myself.

Lydia shuddered. "The sixth of April? It can't be…"

I looked at Lydia, an eyebrow raised.

She shook her head. "That was the day they… Dad and Mom… died, you know."

Quite frankly she was blinking back tears.

"Oh Lia," I said softly. "That's truly terrible."

Cody nodded in agreement, sympathy written all over his face.

Lydia sighed heavily. "But… why is this in here? Shouldn't your mother have it?"

"I should think so," I said, shrugging.

Kodiak stood up a little straighter.

"I think I may know."

"What?" Lia and I asked instantly.

"If I remember correctly," the strawberry-blond boy began, "you were both having a sleepover, right? On the night that it happened?"

I nodded yes.

"Well… Mrs. Arlington likely had gone to the bus and wrote the note by the photo while Lydia was at your house, Fay. Then, she tucked them in one of the books—maybe she was reading the one they were tucked in—and intended to deliver the note the next day, when she went to take Lia home. However, she never got the chance because… because…" Cody's voice trailed off, and we both knew what he meant.

"That makes sense. Perfect sense, actually," Lydia said, though upset. "Oh, Mother…"

The theory seemed quite reliable. But what had caused Mrs. Arlington to write the note to begin with? Why had Father been upset?

Not wanting to dwell long on gloomy thoughts of her parents' death, Lydia changed the subject. "What do the photo and note mean, though?"

"Lia," I said, "may I have the photo and

note? I... I think I should show it to Mother. After all, she was supposed to receive the note so long ago..."

"Of course, Fay," Lydia said, handing it to me. "It was a comfort, though, to see Mother's own handwriting. I'm sure your mother will feel the same."

"Yes," I said. "Mother was so fond of Mrs. Arlington."

Lydia smiled softly. "I'll see you at five this evening."

I had almost forgotten about the sleepover.

"Oh! Yes, goodbye—I really must be going. See you at five, Lydia."

I waved to both Cody and Lia, turned around, and hurried home.

\* \* \*

"Mother!" I shouted, quickly shutting the front door and picking up Gracie, who woofed happily.

"I'm in the kitchen, Felicia dear. Did you have an enjoyable time at school?"

I entered the kitchen.

"Yes, I did, thank you. But really, I must show you something."

Mother turned around from putting spices in a pot of soup, giving me her full attention. "Mm-hmm?"

My heart thumped a bit.

"It's this," I said, and I gently handed her the photo and small letter written on the elegant paper.

"Why, Fay! I remember having that photo taken like it was yesterday." She smiled as she said this, completely happy at such a memory.

"But Mother, look—there's a note too. I think you were supposed to get this three and a half years ago."

My mom turned the photograph over in her hands and gasped sharply.

"Where did you get this, Felicia?" she inquired, choked up.

My friends and I kept the bus a secret—even from our family members, with the exceptions of Lia's grandmother and Cody's brother, Ryker.

I wanted to be truthful but also respect our secret. "Well, I can't really say, Mother. It's kind of a secret between Cody, Lia, and me. But anyway, Lydia found it."

Respecting my wishes, Mother did not inquire further about where the photo and note of long ago had been discovered.

"Oh, my dear Liliana... She was a lovely friend," Mother said, swallowing a lump down her throat. "Do you remember her well, Fay?"

"Yes, I do. I always thought she was so nice, like an auntie or something. I remember at Lia's old house, Mrs. Arlington would make lemon meringue pie from their own lemon trees. And I remember she loved yellow, picnics, and quilting."

I felt a lump in my own throat as I reflected

on the memories.

"But," I said, "I've always wished I could remember *more.*"

"I know, darling. I'm sure you *all* do."

We both sat down on a couple of chairs.

"Mom? Do you feel that way sometimes? Like… you wish you could go back to the past?"

"Yes, I do."

"With Sage?"

"Mm-hmm, and others."

"I always find myself wondering what it would be like if things had ended up differently, you know, like if Sage was still alive—what it would be like."

"I'm sure that's how Lydia feels at times as well, with her parents."

I nodded in agreement but didn't say anything.

"But," Mother began, "no one can change the past. There comes a time in everyone's life when they simply must move on. It's also good to be thankful for what you do have. Sometimes when I feel bad, I think about the things I still have—a wonderful husband, two beautiful daughters, and good friends."

I smiled. The mention of Father, however, reminded me of a question I had longed to ask.

"But Mother, how come in the note Mrs. Arlington says Father was sad?"

Mother sighed and didn't speak for a long time.

"Oh Felicia," she said, folding her hands and putting them in her lap. "Reece—your father—he wasn't always the way he is now."

My eyes widened, and I felt nervous.

"What do you mean, Mother?"

She was quiet for a moment.

"What I'm about to tell you, Felicia, is in the past, okay? This was a long time ago."

I nodded my head, my heart rate quickening. "All right, Mother."

She took a deep breath, and then said, "A long time ago, your father got himself into a bit of a mess. He... he used to break into buildings and steal."

I gasped. For me, it was as if everything stopped for a moment. I couldn't think.

"Father was a thief?" I exclaimed.

"Yes, darling, he *was,* but know that was years ago—when he was a teenager—and he deeply regrets ever doing so."

"How old was he?" I asked, my eyes wide and sad. Father—*my* father, whom I had always respected and loved—had been a thief?

"I suppose he was about sixteen."

"But why, Mother? What made him want to steal?"

"A lot of it had to do with peer pressure, I guess. He had a talent for stealth, and even though he had good friends, he also got mixed up in the wrong kind of crowd, and they pressured him to put his slyness to use."

I nodded slowly. "I can't believe it."

Mother smiled sympathetically.

"I couldn't either, way back then when I first heard. Ever since I had known him, he had always been such a sweet boy, so I just couldn't believe that he of all people was... was a..." she trailed off. "But please remember that that was years ago and that he's regretted it ever since. That's why Liliana wrote me the note. I remember clearly now that Reece had been so depressed shortly before Liliana and Seth died. His past just kept coming back to haunt him."

I nodded, my heart thumping in my chest. "I know Father would never do something like that again. It's just a shock, that's all. I love him just the same."

"It's been years now, and he's been crime-free, so we've nothing to fear. He's become a respected member of society again."

"Oh, yes, Mother!" I said, nodding firmly. "People can change, and I know without a shadow of a doubt that Father has done so."

Mother smiled softly, and we talked a little longer before she went to finish the soup.

As I rose to assist her, I couldn't help but reflect on my family and how there were things even I hadn't known.

# SLEEPOVER CATASTROPHE

## Chapter 6

It was just so hard to believe that Father could have ever been a thief, that he could have broken into places—that he could have been a *criminal*.

But it was true. My mind had wandered a little bit off and on once Lydia came over, but I was grateful to have a friend near during this shocking time, even if she was completely unaware of what I discovered.

Currently, the two of us were playing up in my room.

We were having a tea party and pretending we were fine, grown-up ladies. Mother had even let me borrow the china teacups, saucers, and teapot.

"Mrs. Nobleman," I began, "would you—"

"Mrs. Nobleman?" Lydia inquired.

"Why yes, of course," I said. "You know, Mother always invites ladies over for tea, and since we're pretending we're grown up, you're married."

"Mrs. *Nobleman?*" Lydia asked again. "Am I married to…?"

Her cheeks flushed.

"Cody, of course," I said. "Now, Mrs. Nobleman, would you like one sugar cube, or two?"

"One," replied Lia. I plinked it into her teacup.

Gently stirring the sugar into her tea, Lydia asked with a bit of a humored snort, "Is your husband well?"

"Oh yes, quite," I replied.

"Fay," Lia asked in a whisper and not sounding like an adult, "who's your husband supposed to be?"

"Ryker," I said. "We're sisters-in-law!"

Lydia laughed. It was the same laugh she gave when she thought something was silly—weird even—but still found it amusing.

"Well, uh, Mrs. Nobleman," she said, seeming to feel strange that we both had the same last name, "thank you very much for inviting me over to your home."

"Oh, of course. Would you like a petit four?"

"Yes, thank you."

Mother even had let me make petit fours, a type of small confectionery, for the occasion, much to my delight.

"Oh!" I exclaimed. "I forgot to turn on the music."

I got up and twisted my music box, then set it back down, placing the object on the table. "There."

"I really must have you over for tea soon; I shall bake mini lemon meringue pies, and perhaps some scones."

"Oh yes, indeed. You make a most lovely lemon meringue pie. So tell me, Mrs. Nobleman, what have you been doing? Have you been working on your sampler?"

"Oh yes, I have been working on mine," Lydia said. "I'm nearly finished now, you see, but I'm not yet done, for I am adding some last few details tomorrow. Perhaps I will show you the finished project when I have you over for tea."

"Certainly."

We continued in this manner for a while longer, pretending to be all grown up. But when we heard the doorbell, Lia and I were both curious and thumped down the stairs.

Father opened the door just at the moment Lia and I were on the last couple of stairsteps.

In the doorway were two men—lawmen.

"Hello," one of them said cordially. He had a

full-face beard and dark-blue eyes. "I presume you are Mr. Reece Blackwood?"

"Yes," Father said. "How may I help you?"

"If you could just step outside, please," the cordial lawman said. "We would like a moment to speak to you—in private."

He tilted his head toward Lydia and me as he said the last part of his sentence since we were still standing on the stairs.

"Yes, of course," Father said.

He calmly walked out and then gently shut the door.

Mother appeared in the hall. "Felicia, who was at the door?"

"*Lawmen,*" I said. "They wanted to talk to Father."

Mom's face turned incredibly surprised.

"Girls," she said, "I think it's best you both go back upstairs for now."

I nodded. "Yes, Mother, of course."

Lydia also nodded and politely went upstairs with me, the two of us going back into my room.

"What do you think they want?" I asked Lia, my eyes growing wide.

"I don't know, Fay—hopefully nothing."

We were both quiet, and then Lydia suddenly burst out, "Oh, *Fay!* Suppose it's about the robbery that took place in Wilsonville. Maybe they think Mr. Blackwood was a witness and that he can help them solve the case, or maybe they're asking Uriah's friends."

I just shrugged, for I was dreadfully nervous and my hands were shaking. I started pacing.

*What if they think…?*

Not willing to finish the thought, I shook my head vigorously, which resulted in Lydia giving me a perplexed look.

"Why, Felicia, what's wrong? You're very pale."

"It's just…"

"…just what?"

"Personal."

Lydia didn't inquire any further.

Suddenly we heard the sound of footsteps thumping up the stairs. It wasn't much longer before I saw the two lawmen.

"Excuse us," said the cordial one, "but we're searching the house."

"Y-You're what?" I said, shocked.

"You'll have to pardon us, miss," he replied. "It's part of our job."

They looked around the room carefully, though I don't think they expected to find anything in my girly, pink room.

The one who hadn't spoken yet picked up the music box—and surprisingly gently, searched it for any supposed clues, though I really wasn't sure why. I mean, it didn't seem likely there would be anything significant in a music box. It wasn't as if they would find a million dollars or anything!

He put it back down after his careful search.

Both men were polite, and so that put me at ease somewhat. Of course, they wouldn't falsely accuse Father of anything with no evidence—right?

"Thank you for your cooperation," the bearded lawman said.

I couldn't do anything more than just give a nod, and then the two men walked out of my room to search the rest of the house.

Lydia and I exchanged shocked stares.

"That just… happened," she said.

Again, I nodded… at last, bursting out, "I-I can't believe it…!"

The two of us were shocked into silence, and several minutes went by.

Unexpectedly, we heard footsteps again and turned our heads to the noise.

*Are they back to search?*

The maker of the sound was soon revealed to be none other than my own father.

"F-Father!" I exclaimed.

"My dear Felicia…" he began and came over to me, his voice soft and mild.

"What is it, Father?" I asked, feeling a horrible dread sweep over me.

As if knowing this was going to be a personal conversation, Lydia said she would excuse us and quietly walked into the hallway.

"What is it?" I inquired again, this time more

urgent.

Father knelt down a little bit to be more at my eye level.

"I have to go, Funnel Cake," he said in a whisper.

"What?" I asked, my voice quiet but sharp.

"I didn't do anything," he said, "but they want me to come with them, just because they are being careful and are a bit suspicious. Lynette told that me she let you know about... about the past, so I know you know what they are thinking. They're willing to let me tell you goodbye, but I must leave soon."

"No!" I said. "You *can't* leave."

The tears were springing up into my blue eyes. Like I've said before, I tended to have a bit of a temper on occasion; however, there wasn't any anger today—only shock and utter sadness. Now wasn't the time to be angry.

"I'll be back," he whispered, his voice brave and strong. "I love you."

I crushed Father in a tight hug, as if it would somehow prevent him from leaving.

"I love you too," I whispered back. "Come back fast."

"I'll try. Goodbye, Felicia Jade."

"Goodbye, Father. I'll miss you terribly."

"As will I miss you, Funnel Cake. But now is the time to be brave."

He gave me one more hug and then turned to

leave. But then, spinning on his heel, said quickly, "One more thing—Miles Carpenter is still to work on things at the office. Make sure he knows for me, okay?"

I nodded largely, and Father smiled gently despite his troubles.

"I must leave, but I'll come home should the Lord will. Have faith and hope."

In a moment he was gone, and my life was turned upside down.

\* \* \*

*"One more thing—Miles Carpenter is still to work on things at the office. Make sure he knows for me, okay?"*

Father's words resonated in my mind, retelling me what I needed to do. Of course, Miles couldn't manage everything like a professional eye doctor could, but he could still be of much assistance.

It was three days after Father's horrible departure. I felt empty—numb to any emotion except utter depression—and quite frankly didn't see the point in getting to school on time or doing much of anything productive.

Just four days earlier had been my thirteenth birthday, and just three days ago, my father had been snatched away from me—possibly forever. The tears began to slide down my face, a feeling of hopelessness sinking into every bone in my body.

My mind was running in circles, and I would have stayed in my room all day had not my dear mother called me down.

Now I will say that if one thing helped me immensely, it was the fact that Lydia had been there when it all happened, and seeing as she was one of my two best friends, I was truly fortunate to have had her around. She, having undergone her own share of troubles, made a wonderful and relatable comforter, and I think it's important for everyone to have one good friend in life to help them through life's hardships—a friend like Lydia.

I really had no desire to go to school—which would greatly concern anyone who knew me. However, I was shocked by everything that had so quickly happened. I was embarrassed as well, because it was likely I would be unable to hold back my tears at some point, and the kids at school would see it.

But bad—terrible—things happen, and sometimes you have to endure the day. So I walked down the stairs slowly and wiped away the tears I was having trouble managing.

"Hello," was all I said as I entered the kitchen. My voice was flat, I was deprived of much-needed sleep, and I was feeling the tears spring up again. It's hard to talk when you're miserable.

"Hello Felicia," Mother said with a gentle smile. "I hope you will have a fine day at school."

Mother was being incredibly brave over the whole situation, knowing she must still go on about her housework, and all for her family. I was certain she intended to leave after we left for school, to find out more news concerning my father and speak to him if possible. She had tried to on Saturday, but was unable, and had tried on Sunday, but had no luck then either.

"Thank you, Mother. And I hope you and Leanne are well while I'm away."

To be honest, I was scared to leave the house. If they could come in and take Father away, what if they would take Mother and Leanne away from me too? It didn't make sense, really, seeing as Mother didn't have a bad past with the law and Leanne was a baby, but then again, my mom *was* married to a former criminal.

"Thank you, darling. Now, we must get to breakfast so you won't be late for school."

Mother was hiding her pain, I was sure. She was the most amazing mother ever and was trying to keep her spirits up for my sake.

I wasn't hungry at all. Having breakfast today was just a chore I did because it had to be done and there was no point in skipping it.

We left for school, and when we arrived, she dropped me off, saying she would be back in time to pick me up—but that if something prevented her, to ask Lydia's grandmother to take me home. After a quick goodbye hug, she drove off.

Interestingly, Cody hadn't found out what had happened yet, because I hadn't seen him since we were at the bus. He, his mother, and Ryker had all been sick with colds, and Cody's father had been out of town, and so none of them had been at church on Sunday. I remembered Cody sneezing a few times on Friday, so I hadn't been too surprised to discover he was ill. He had allergies sometimes, though, so he probably thought he was fine then, until the rest of the cold symptoms set in.

As I approached the building, I saw that he was indeed back at school, so he must have been feeling better. Lydia appeared to have not yet arrived, though.

Cody grinned when he saw me and waved me over.

"Hi, Fay!" he chirped. "Ugh, I haven't seen you in *forever.* I was stuck at home all of Saturday and Sunday with some cold. My nose was *so* stuffy, but I couldn't stop sneezing! I just about sneezed my head completely off! And then I gave my cold to Ryker, and then he gave it to Mom, and I guess it's good Dad was gone on business anyway, because Mom would have probably given it to him, and that would've been rotten."

Cody was as bright and happy as usual, even though he sounded a little stuffed up still. His sunniness made even *me* feel better from my miserable predicament.

I smiled softly at him, and this only caused his grin to grow.

"Well, I'm glad you're feeling much better," I said, my voice somewhat weak from sorrow and lack of sleep, but sincere nonetheless.

Kodiak could instantly tell something was up by the tone of my voice, and his hazel eyes grew very wide.

"Why, Fay!" he exclaimed. "What's wrong?"

My eyes got watery. I couldn't help it, and I turned away.

I just wanted to pretend nothing had happened about Father. I wanted to listen to my friend go on and on in his cheery manner, and then talk to Lydia about... about anything but this.

"Oh Cody," I said, my voice filled with melancholy. "Father's... Father's gone!"

Through my tears, I could see Cody's eyes get very wide.

"Wait... He's *what?*" he asked, confused and concerned.

"*Gone!*" I repeated, my voice getting a little louder.

Of course, Kodiak had known that was what I said. He just had no way of understanding what I meant by "gone."

"Gone where?" he inquired gently.

It took me a moment to speak again. "Gone... gone to... Taken away..."

It was at this moment that Lydia arrived, and upon seeing my woeful state, she knew right away what the conversation was about.

Cody helplessly said to Lia, "Fay's saying something about her father having gone someplace, but I don't know where."

Lydia, taking Kodiak aside by a couple of feet, whispered to him. While over at my house for the sleepover, Lydia had learned some of my Father's backstory, though it hadn't been easy for me to tell her, and so she was well equipped to explain what happened.

Cody's eyes grew wide.

"That's terrible!" he exclaimed. "He *has* to come back."

I let out a shaky sigh. "And he will."

"I'm really sorry, Felicia," Kodiak said, shuddering a bit. "I can hardly imagine it."

But the bell rang, so the three of us quietly walked into our class.

* * *

After school, Mother picked me up, and we drove to Father's eye doctor's office. Miles needed to know his new responsibilities, after all.

"So, Mother," I began after I got into the truck and shut the door, "did you find anything out about Father?"

She nodded. "I did."

Mom carefully pulled out of the school parking lot and then resumed the conversation.

"The reason they took him away is—as I suspected, of course—because he has a criminal record."

"Yeah, but he's been good for years!"

"I know. But he would be more suspicious than the average person."

I nodded.

"Well Fay, they think he may have been the person who committed the robbery in Wilsonville not too long ago."

"But that's insane—Father would *never!*"

"Well, he did in the past, and that's all they remember. Again, *I* know he wouldn't do it; but *they* don't know that. They're not saying it *is* him, just that it *might* be. To them, he's a likely suspect, and so they want him over at the jail for a little while."

"They can't put Father in jail," I said.

"Well, I suppose they can or something, because they already have," Mother said.

I was scared. Mom must have noticed because she reassuringly added, "But don't worry, Felicia. Your father is innocent, and they'll believe that soon enough. I'm confident."

But *I* wasn't, and I'm ashamed to say it. Sure, I knew Father didn't commit the crime, but how could I get *them* to believe that? If only there was a way! There *had* to be.

I sat in silence for a while, and then the determined realization dawned on me.

*I'll just have to find out who did do it and prove*

*Father to be an honorable man.*

Now it was only a matter of how.

* * *

When we arrived at the eye doctor's office, I easily found my way to Father's part of the building, knocked on his office door, and waited a moment.

I heard some shuffling around and then, "Hello? Come in."

Swinging open the door, I said, "Hello Miles."

"Why hello, Felicia. Hey, I'm really sorry to hear about Mr. Blackwood. They'll find him to be innocent; I'm sure of it."

He looked a little sad.

I nodded. "Yes. Speaking of Father, that's why I am here. You see, Dad specifically told me to inform you that you are to take care of things here while he's away."

Miles widened his eyes in surprise.

"Really? That's... I can't believe he trusts me so much, to be able to manage things for him. I'm honored."

I smiled a bit. "Of course. He seems to think very highly of you."

"Well, thank you, Felicia. The only problem is that I'm working another job at the moment, too."

I tilted my head. "Really? So, will you not be able to take care of things here then?"

This was certainly unexpected.

*Who will temporarily take Father's place if Miles can't?*

"Oh, I want to work here very much," he said quickly. "But I'm not sure if I'll be able to. I'll ask the boss today, though, and hope for the best."

"Where are you working, Mr. Carpenter?"

"The bank."

"Wow, really? I thought your brother was going to work there possibly. How did you end up doing it?"

Miles laughed lightly. "The banker told me to give it a try and tell him if I thought it was a good bank. I was looking for a job anyway, to make some extra income, you know. I bought a really tiny house that my roommate and I are splitting the costs for, but I'm kind of not doing so well, financially speaking."

"Oh, I had no idea!"

I didn't know much about Miles.

"So," he continued, "I was going to find a job anyway, and the banker's been paying pretty well. If I can get my brother to move here, I'll get a job elsewhere. But now with your father needing some help, I think I'll be seeing if I can shorten my hours at the bank."

"Oh, we'll pay you to help here, of course, Mr. Carpenter," I said. "And Father will be very grateful."

Miles nodded a little.

"I'll check with the banker as soon as I go there today. Say, Felicia?"

"Hmm?"

"Uh, never mind."

"You can tell me. What is it?"

"Don't worry about it. I'll see you around."

I hesitated. "Okay, then. Goodbye."

Shutting the door, I left and returned to my mother, who was at the front desk talking with the woman who worked here.

"Oh yes, thank you, Eliza."

"Any time, ma'am."

Mother smiled and turned to me. "Ready, Felicia?"

"Almost," I replied. "Do you mind if I linger here a bit? I'm wanting to do a little research."

"Go ahead; I'll be in the truck. I need to make some adjustments to my shopping list, anyway."

Mother left, and I turned back to the front desk.

"Eliza," I said, "can I look at some old papers."

"That would depend on the papers, I guess," she said with a bit of a smile.

"Do you have any of the old ones saved from when people were scheduled for appointments?"

"I'll see what I have." She pulled open a drawer and searched around. I eyed the lobby as I waited.

"Okay, I have papers here from the last two weeks or so. I don't know why I hadn't thrown them out."

"Thank you." I searched through the papers, looking at each date.

"Eliza?"

"Yes?"

I took a double look through the papers.

"There isn't any paper for the twentieth of August."

The woman looked carefully at my stack, and then looked in the drawer.

"That's strange. Hmm, I don't know what happened... Sorry, Fay."

"I really need that one, too..." I replied.

"Sorry," she said again, giving me a sympathetic look.

It was true that I needed it badly. On the twentieth of August, a Friday, Father had been away on a business trip and didn't return until Saturday evening. Now the night of the robbery had been uncertain, but it had occurred in the time frame of the twentieth to the twenty-third. If by using the paper, I could prove that Father had no appointments on the twentieth, that would have at least helped give him a defense, an alibi. It would help prove he hadn't been in Wilsonville, anyway.

*I'll just have to keep looking for clues. But... what if that one paper was the piece of the puzzle we can't live without?*

# Kodiak's Valor

## Chapter 7

"So how ya doing, Fay?"

I turned my head to my strawberry-blond friend.

"I'm fine, Cody," I said with a small smile. "It's just Father who isn't."

He smiled softly back.

We were at Lydia's house, homework piled on the kitchen table, a platter of sugar cookies in front of us, and a glass of strawberry milk by each of our spots.

"The eye doctor's office didn't have the *one* paper I needed."

Shooting me a sympathetic look, Lydia said, "There's got to be some other form of evidence—I'm sure of it."

I rested my face on my hand, thinking and sipping my milk. The strawberry flavor was the best—well, it made the milk pink, so that was already a given.

"Whoever *did* commit the robbery could still be *in* Wilsonville."

Cody nodded, also thinking deeply. "Mm-hmm. We can—and should—all keep an eye out for anything suspicious."

Lydia sat up a little straighter. "Absolutely. And if we can find out who *really* did it, then we can prove Mr. Blackwood innocent."

"So," I said, "there are two things that need to be done: Find proof of Father's innocence and find out who really did commit the crime. But... how do we go about achieving those?"

All three of us were silent, pondering.

"Wait!" Lydia burst out.

Cody and I turned our attention to Lia instantly. "What?"

"I don't know why I didn't think of this earlier—we should talk to Uriah!"

"Oh, Lia!" I shouted. "Of course. What a great idea!"

Cody beamed, sipping his strawberry milk

through his blue- and orange-striped straw. "Really, that was an amazing idea, Lia. No doubt Uriah's already looking into the case. He's so *cool!*"

Lydia nodded wholeheartedly.

"I second that," she said. "He's a real live private detective!"

"So, we'll ask him tomorrow?" I inquired.

"Ugh," Cody said. "I can't tomorrow."

"Why not?"

"I've got my regular chores plus helping Dad break a horse, baking snickerdoodles, and then company all evening."

"Good point—especially the one about the snickerdoodles," I replied with a laugh. "Okay, we can do it the day after tomorrow, then. Meanwhile, keep an eye out, and I'll see if I can find any information."

"I'll do the same," Lydia said.

"I don't know how much I can find out as far as clues go when I'm breaking a horse, but okay."

I smiled. "What would I ever do without you guys?"

* * *

The next day, Mother and I left to visit Natasha and baby Owen. We hadn't seen them for a while and wanted to know how things were fairing.

"Hello, Lynette. Hi, Felicia. How are you girls today? I'm so sorry about Reece. I'm confident they'll find him innocent."

"Yes," Mother said gently, "I'm sure of it, too. But how are you, Natasha? And Owen?"

A lovely smile enveloped Natasha's face.

"Oh, just lovely! Here, sit down and have some bread—it's fresh from the oven. You see, things have been looking up. It's been pretty crazy around here, but we're fine. Will's been doing some odd jobs here and there—mowing lawns, that kind of thing—but he also got a nice, though temporary, job at a nursing home. They keep him working pretty late some nights, but we're very thankful."

"That's wonderful," Mother replied. "And Owen's doctor's appointments?"

Natasha's smile wavered a bit. "Though things have been better as far as affording them, the medical plans are rather expensive for us still. We'll figure out something, though."

Mother nodded. "We'd be happy to help—"

"I know, Lynette, but you know how Will is. He won't accept charity from anyone."

"Friends help friends, though," my mother replied with her gentle smile.

"Of course, but you know Will. We'll manage—we always have."

She looked a little concerned as she said so, though.

The gloom on Natasha's face vanished away,

however, upon seeing her son wake up.

"Oh, look!" she said with a beam, sweetly. "Owen's awake and ready to visit."

She lifted him out of his bassinet, and he cooed, making my heart melt.

"Hi, Owen," I chirped, holding out my finger. I melted even more when he gripped it.

"He's so cute," I said fondly.

"Thank you," Natasha replied. "He seems to like you a lot."

"And *I* love babies," I said. "They're always so cute—almost always, anyway. I'm going to have ten of them one day, when I'm all grown up."

The two adults laughed.

"Wow," Natasha said. "I can't necessarily say I disagree with you, though. I love them, too. Maybe you can babysit Owen when he's a bit older, hmm?"

I nodded very enthusiastically.

"Please!"

Mother beamed at me. "I think you have the same mind as your great-grandmother. You know, my mother was one of twelve!"

Natasha sighed delightedly. "Oh, *Lynette!* You must tell me more about France. Please do."

With a little laugh, Mom agreed. She went on to tell us about her early life in Paris, about her favorite French bakery; the colorful macarons they sold; the long, delicious baguettes; and so on. She explained how bright it was outside on summer nights—there was still much light out after she went to bed—and so many other things.

I love listening to Mother talk about her homeland. Learning about other places is so interesting! Around that time, she was teaching me various French recipes to bake, as well as songs on the piano. I wanted to learn to sing the various songs, but I wasn't fluent in the language like she still was. I knew I could become fluent, though, if I tried hard enough. There were some sentences I could form, but it was a long way coming.

At eight years old, Mother had immigrated from her big city in France all the way to our tiny home of Wilsonville, Nebraska. What a change! But she said she had always heard about America because her father was an American, after all, so she wasn't afraid.

"Besides," Mother said with a smirk, "if I hadn't moved to America, I would have never met Reece. He was from Los Angeles, you know, so I guess we both came from pretty big cities. Who would have thought we'd both move to this little, yet lovely, Wilsonville!"

We chatted about various things, and Owen peacefully fell asleep in Natasha's arms. Smiling, Natasha then looked from me to Mother, the sight of her son reminding her of something.

"Can you two keep a secret?"

"Of course!" we chirped.

"Whenever Owen is taking his nap and I've finished my housework, I crochet hot pads and blankets and things, so I can sell them at the farmers' market in Cambridge. I'm trying to help with the income a bit, for the medicine and all. It's a surprise for Will—I know he'll be delighted."

"That's so sweet," Mother said. "We could help you, you know. Fay and I love to crochet."

"Oh, yes!" I nearly sang.

"I'd like that, yet I'm not sure how Will would feel. You know how he is about charity."

Mother, brightening up the room with her smile like usual, said, "Well, my hot pads are well worn out by now. So, I do believe *I'll* be needing to buy some of yours. And we'll just have to see what else you'll be selling, too."

The last sentence she said with a playful look on her face.

I giggled, and Natasha beamed, laughing in delight.

"Lynette, you're so sweet."

Cheerily, I noticed that spending time with Natasha and her adorable baby helped me to not feel so sad about all that had been happening lately.

\* \* \*

"Oh, hi, Felicia. How are you doing?"

98

"Fine, thank you, Justice."

I was at school the next day. Things had been going decently enough. Surprisingly, there hadn't been too much talk at school about me and my father—as far as I could tell, anyway—and I was pretty relieved about that.

Amity gave me a sympathetic look. "Have you found anything out about Mr. Blackwood?"

"Not really," I said.

Justice nodded. "I really hope things go well. It must be a pretty frightening feeling. Amity and I can relate."

"You can?" I asked, tilting my head.

"Yeah," Amity said, a bit of an awkward look crossing her face. "Let's just say we may have been to court at some point in our lives."

"Wait, really?"

Justice slightly laughed. "Yeah, it's kind of an interesting story. Our neighbor sued us over cheesecake."

He sighed as he said the sentence, and Cody, who had just joined in on the conversation, burst out laughing—which wasn't that fitting for the moment, but even I'll admit it sounded ridiculous in a slightly humorous way.

"How?" the strawberry-blond boy asked.

Amity blushed. "She—our neighbor at the time—was allergic to one of the ingredients in a cheesecake we baked, and we gave her the cake without knowing she had an allergy. She had a reaction and sued us. It was really crazy. But yeah, unfortunately, we lost the lawsuit and had to pay a large fine, all for what was supposed to be a good deed."

"That's terrible!" I said.

"Yes, it was. However," Justice began, reassuringly, "I'm sure things will get figured out with your father, Fay."

"I've been praying about it often," Amity said.

I smiled. "Thanks, that means a lot."

Smiling back, Amity said, "Of course."

The twins were very nice, but before we could continue any further discussion, the bell rang loudly, making Cody and me shout out a "Bye!" and then hurry to our next class.

* * *

"So," Lydia said, sitting down at our usual table for lunch, "the plan's initiated today, eh? Stumbled upon any evidence?"

I shook my head. "Nothing."

"Me neither," Kodiak said, then with a slight laugh continued, "I don't suppose one can expect to just 'stumble upon' evidence and—boom—solve a mystery just like that!"

"That's a valid statement," I replied.

"Ryker says even a broken clock is right every

now and then."

Lydia furrowed her eyebrows a little bit, having an amused grin on her face. "He calls you a broken clock?"

"I guess so."

"Well," I began, "talking to Uriah will count as *searching* for evidence, rather than 'stumbling' upon it. So that's good."

We were about to further discuss our plan when Cody's face turned white with dread.

"Oh, *no!*" he exclaimed and then attempted to push me down under the table, whispering. "Watch out, it's Trevin!"

He hissed for Lia to hide and then started to duck under the table himself before I stopped him.

"Hey!" I said. "Remain calm, Kodiak! It's just Trevin."

My last sentence caused Cody to stare at me in utter shock with his jaw dropped, as if I had just spoken treason to him and hate against snickerdoodles or something.

I mean, sure, I didn't like being around Trevin, but he wasn't a complete monster, either.

"How can you say, 'just Trevin'!" Cody exclaimed—though still whispering—to me. "Felicia Jade Blackwood, there is no such thing as 'just Trevin.' Unless you feel as calm as a clam about how I got pushed in a locker back in third grade, or at perfect ease over how he embarrassed me—really, really bad—on the final day of sixth grade earlier this year, he isn't 'just Trevin.' Surely you're not okay with that!"

"Hello, Cody," Trevin said, smirking his usual smirk.

Cody was silent but wouldn't take his eyes off the bully.

Trevin then turned to me. "And hello, Felicia."

Cody looked a little defensive of me, scooting his chair an inch closer.

"So, how've ya been, Kodiak?"

*Trevin didn't even acknowledge Lydia's existence—ouch. Not that he's necessarily trying to be nice by acknowledging ours, though.*

"I'm fine," Cody replied stiffly.

Trevin, holding his head up a bit high, said, "I'm just here to give Felicia my condolences. I'm sorry to hear about your father and am positive he's innocent. See? That's all, Kodiak. You don't have to look so defensive, you know. What is it with you, anyway? You don't like me talking to Felicia?"

Cody seemed to be gritting his teeth.

Trevin shrugged. "Well, I'll be on my way. See you around. And oh, by the way, I had a really wonderful time at your house when I was over last month, Felicia."

I heard Cody gasp sharply, and I realized what

Trevin had just done.

*Oh no…! Trevin…*

I was sure he had let that little piece of information slip out on purpose. My fists clenched while my temper rose.

*Nice going, Trevin!* I thought sarcastically.

Trevin smirked at me before turning to Lia.

"Oh, and sorry to have ignored you, Lydia. I didn't see you there. You sure were quiet today."

*Oh, I'm sure you saw her.*

Having said his piece, he spun on his heel and left, and I felt as if I could see his smirk as he did so.

Lydia let out a heavy sigh.

"That was 'interesting'; it always is, when Trevin's involved."

"Yeah…" I said, blushing a bit.

Why did Trevin always have to come in and ruin everything? Cody was right—you never could say, "just Trevin"!

Lia likely knew there must have been a good explanation for why such a bully had been at my house, and so she didn't seem to be concerned. "We just have to not pay any attention to him, that's all," she said.

Cody was silent.

\* \* \*

At first, I thought maybe I could just ignore Trevin spilling the beans about being at my house, and just act as if nothing had ever been said about it. But Cody was obviously confused and upset—and for good reason, knowing the way Trevin Aragon was. I knew the only way to fix things was to… well, to bring it up.

So, when we were walking outside, I finally got up the nerve to turn to my strawberry-blond friend and face him.

Lydia seemed to always know how to handle these tricky situations and had whispered to me earlier that day that she was sure I had a good explanation for what Trevin said, and that maybe Cody and I should sort things out between the two of us. Lia said I could always fill her in later.

She left us alone, leaving to hang out with Ryker and Micah, and from what I noticed later, she seemed to be having a pretty good time with the two older teens. It looked like she and Ryker were trying to invent some new secret handshake, laughing a lot in the process.

"Kodiak," I began, "I'm sorry about Trevin. I've got a good explanation for it."

"You had him over at your house?" Cody looked at me, his hazel eyes wide. "Are you guys great buddies or something?"

I stared at my friend, and then burst out laughing.

"Me and Trevin, great friends?" I exclaimed. "Don't be ridiculous! I only had him over because

Mother said so."

"You did?"

Cody let out a huge sigh of relief.

"I was worried you were secretly hanging out with him or something!"

"I will be honest, he actually wasn't that bad most of the time when he was at my house, but he was only there because we had to work on that project together, and Mother said for me to invite him."

Cody looked at me in earnest, but I stopped him before he could say anything.

"Trevin Aragon is rude and I'm certainly not blind to that. You've nothing to fear, Cody."

Any sign of past distress vanished from his face. "Thanks, Fay."

"So," I said, "are you ready to go encounter Uriah?"

"You know it."

* * *

About an hour later, my two best friends and I walked up Uriah's driveway and over to his front door. Cody gave three clear, loud knocks, and then we waited.

"His doorbell broke, and he hasn't gotten around to fixing it yet, or else I'd ring that," Kodiak explained.

Lydia nodded. "He's probably been too busy

with his criminal cases."

We waited about thirty more seconds, but to no avail, so Cody knocked again, this time even louder.

I looked at my two friends.

"Perhaps he's out buying groceries or something."

"I'm thinking we should have called first," Cody said.

"Probably."

*I should have thought of that,* I realized, and felt a little embarrassed!

"No wait," Lydia responded. "I saw him at the bank when I was with Grandmother yesterday, right after school, and I said the three of us were planning to see him after school today if that was okay. Remember? That's what I said at lunch. He told me that was fine, so he should be here, right?"

"Maybe something came up and he forgot to let us know," said Cody.

"Well, he's obviously not here, so I suppose we had better just leave," I told them.

"I guess so," Cody agreed, pushing his bangs away from his eyes.

We turned to leave, but Lydia asked us to stay for a moment.

"What is it, Lia?" I asked.

She went to the left side of the front yard and then went cautiously behind the corner of the house.

Cody followed her to see what was up, and then I, not wanting to be left, joined my friends too.

"Wow," Cody whispered. "Look, his gate's open!"

Quietly walking ahead of Lia, he silently inched his way to the open gate. I could see his hands shaking a little bit, as if nervous as to what he might be about to discover, and I quite frankly couldn't blame him for his nerves.

Reaching the gate, Cody paused. Then, hesitantly, he carefully turned his face to peek through the opened entrance.

Cody let out a sharp gasp, and for a moment everything was still. He didn't move an inch, and I could practically feel his shock.

At last, he turned to us and said softly, "Girls? Wait for me, okay? Don't follow; just wait."

He then slipped into the backyard, and every muscle in my body told me to go and see what was wrong, but I remembered his words and trusted.

Lydia looked as if she were about to dart after him too, but she planted her feet firmly to the ground.

My heart was pounding because, although I knew Kodiak had a good reason for acting the way he did, I didn't like not knowing what was going on.

"If he doesn't return in another minute, I'm going," I said, sounding somewhat brave, though I certainly didn't feel like I was. After all, Cody was the one in the backyard—not me.

Lydia nodded. "I'm going too."

Silently and carefully, I counted the seconds in my head, and at fifty, my friend returned, his face rather pale but not horrified beyond measure.

"Okay," he said. "You can come if you want. I was making sure no one was still there; the windows are busted, so... so I'm sure he's also been a victim of robbery."

I gasped.

"Kodiak, are you serious?"

He nodded. "I'm afraid so."

"Oh no..." Lydia said, her face white. "Did you check the inside?"

Cody stood up a little straighter. "No. I'm going to, though. You guys don't need to come, just in case it's dangerous, you know."

"No!" Lydia burst out. "I'm going."

"Then I am as well," I replied.

"Fine," Cody said, looking a little uncertain. "I'll stay in the front though, just in case."

I knew he had an inner strength inside that meant he was willing to put himself in danger if it helped protect anyone he cared about. It was as if it was a natural instinct for him, and I wondered if he even realized it. One thing, however, was that he had a sense of fear, and to be honest, I appreciated that.

Cody didn't put himself in harm's way for the sake of it. He was valiant but not completely reckless, and really, he was living up to his last name, Nobleman, because truly he *was* noble.

The three of us quietly entered the backyard, and I felt angry upon seeing the shattered glass. It was so wrong!

"Okay, watch your step so you don't get cut," Cody said. "Oh, and don't trip over that brick; I almost did that the first time."

The door was wide open, for I suppose a robber is in so much of a hurry to get out that he doesn't think about such things. Not that he would care anyway.

Cody carefully walked in and flipped the light switch on.

I was relieved to see that the inside was, for the most part, not too messed up.

We carefully walked into the kitchen, didn't see anything interesting, and then walked into the hallway where the bedrooms are.

The three of us carefully looked around the rooms, but things interestingly weren't too ruined— just a few items knocked over in some places.

"Well," Cody began, letting out a relieved sigh, "I guess no one's still in here."

"I'm so thankful," I replied. "And I think I know what to do. Uriah's home phone is in the living room. If we call his cell phone, we can alert him of the robbery, and then he can come and see for himself if anything is missing."

"Sharp as a tack, Fay," Cody said, giving me a slight smile.

The three of us went into the living room. Lydia and I walked to Uriah's coffee table, which had some coasters, a candle, and his home phone on it.

The robber had apparently thrust the drawer of the coffee table open, and I saw some random trinkets and things as well as a photograph that was in the midst of it all.

"Oh Fay, look," Lydia said shakily. "It's a picture of Uriah and… and Miss Caden, stuffed away in his drawer among these knickknacks and all. I can't imagine what he had to go through."

The last part of the sentence she said with a heavy sigh, feeling sorry for the poor detective.

"It must have been so hard on him," I said.

Cody came up to join us, and he also grew sad as he looked at the photograph. He then turned away from us, leaving me to wonder what was going on in his head.

Sighing, I then dialed the phone.

# Oᴨ ᴛHE Liᴨᴇ

## Chapter 8

Uriah had hurried to his burglarized house immediately after I had called him about the news, so we didn't have to wait long at all.

"Mr. Harper," I breathed, "who do you think *did* this?"

He shook his head, fists clenching a bit.

"I have my suspicions."

Cody looked up with raised eyebrows. "Who?"

Almost certainly, whoever robbed Uriah also robbed the other family in Wilsonville. If Uriah knew who it was, Father's innocence could easily be proven, most likely. Who could it be?

"Well," he began, "I would say, but I'm still busy with research. I wouldn't want to falsely accuse anyone."

"Can't you tell us who you think it is, though?" I asked.

He shrugged. "I feel a bit uneasy about it. You see, when I was solving my first case, I assumed too easily that I knew who it was and ended up being wrong."

Lydia and I exchanged glances.

I supposed Uriah had a point.

"Okay," I said, sighing a bit.

"So, how come you guys were here, anyway?"

I was embarrassed to recall we hadn't even explained that part yet.

"I'm trying to prove my father innocent," I explained. "We came to see if we could talk to you—in case you knew anything, that is."

He nodded. "Well, as you know, I'm still searching…" Trailing off, he peered at his wrecked house. "If I can get closer to knowing, I'll be sure to notify you guys. Have you had any luck?"

I shook my head. "I went to my dad's office and tried to get a paper I thought I could use for at least part of an alibi. All the other papers were there, but *it* was missing!"

Uriah looked confused. "Really? That's strange."

"I think it was just thrown away prematurely," I

clarified.

"That… could very well be…"

"But still…" My voice trailed off.

Lydia joined in on the conversation. "Do you have any ideas on how we could search for evidence?" she asked the detective.

Uriah thought for a moment. As his eyes surveyed what had become of his home, he appeared troubled. No wonder, as there certainly must have been a very devoted robber in Wilsonville to have robbed two homes in such a short amount of time!

"Hmm. This is very, very serious business, as you all know. I'm uneasy with the idea of you three thirteen-year-olds searching for evidence about a crime."

I looked at Uriah in earnest. "I know, but *please*. It's my *father* on the line."

Uriah gave me a half smile. "I understand."

"So can't you tell us at least something?" I asked softly.

"Well…" He paused, hesitant. "Okay… fine. I advise you to be *extremely* cautious. I can't stress this enough. Don't assume it's anyone too rashly. Don't give away that you think it's someone. And, don't—I repeat, *don't*—do anything *I* wouldn't do."

Cody shuddered.

"I wouldn't dream of it," he said.

"If you see something suspicious, let me know.

This is my job; let me handle the tricky situations. Don't try anything as dangerous as what I'm trained to handle, because if you do, you're guaranteed for trouble."

Lydia stood a little straighter, taking careful attention to Uriah's every word.

"Where should we start?"

"Well, think like this: Has anyone acted suspicious? What did they do? Who were those closest to them? What motivation could the suspect have to do something wrong?"

"Right," I said.

*If only I had a notepad! Then I could take notes...*

"If you *can* think of someone, search for evidence. But only—*only*—if you can do so safely."

I nodded.

"Okay... Sounds like a plan. Thanks, Mr. Harper."

He smiled slightly, though still appearing worried.

"You're welcome. But remember—don't do *anything* I wouldn't do."

Again, I nodded—all three of us did.

* * *

The next day, my friends and I met up at Kodiak's house. We were enjoying snickerdoodles, which seemed to always be in Cody's kitchen, and were discussing the break-ins.

"Uriah said to recall if anyone's acted suspicious," Lydia reminded us. "I can't think of anyone at the moment—I've been reflecting since yesterday, actually, and still no luck. What about you guys?"

Cody's eyebrows knitted together a bit in concentration, but he shook his head.

"No one seems odd to me. Not even any random strangers I happened to notice."

I nodded in agreement. "Me too…"

My eyes turned to a picture hung on the wall of Leanne, Mother, Father, and me. I stared at it.

"No, wait," I said.

"What is it?" Cody and Lia asked instantly.

Silent, I thought deeply, trying to put any pieces together.

I could hardly bear to continue the idea.

"What?" Cody further inquired, looking at me with his hazel eyes big and curious.

I shook my head a little bit. "Well, it's just… It's just that the only person I can think of who could even be considered is—well, is Miles Carpenter!"

Lydia gasped. "Wait, what makes you say that?"

I shook my head again.

"I don't really have much evidence—it's just… I don't know him very well. He's a newcomer, and therefore there isn't much *anyone* knows about him."

She nodded. "That's true. But of course, we need more evidence than that. What else is there about him? Anything suspicious?"

I thought very carefully, not wanting to say anything against the intern but also knowing we may be on to something.

Cody sat up a bit straighter.

"He works at the bank, right?"

I nodded. "Yeah. What would that have to do with being a thief, though? Wouldn't that be the last place a thief would work at?"

Lia nodded. "You'd think," she said. Then she suddenly burst out, "No, no wait!"

Cody and I turned to her with faces that bid her continue.

"If he's working at the bank, maybe it makes him *look* less suspicious, which is just what he wants. Maybe it'll even make it easier for him to steal from it because he'll be right there—just slip in a dollar here and there or something. Maybe he wanted even more money, so he went for a full-out robbery of a house—or two."

She had a point. But could it really be true? Could my father's intern be the robber all along? There wasn't much evidence at all in support of it, but it was worth contemplating.

I nodded, and Cody sat deep in thought over the news.

"We can't be too rash," he said almost to himself. Then he repeated himself a bit louder and turned his head up to us.

"We can't be too rash."

Letting out a sigh, Lydia replied, "Of course, but still… I can't think of a person in the world that it could be if he's not the one."

Agreeing, I said, "Neither can I. I just hate the thought, though. He always seems so nice."

Cody shook his head firmly. "We have to be careful; that's what Uriah said."

"We will be, Cody," Lydia said. "He's just a suspect, that's all."

Just a suspect. I let out a slight laugh because she sounded so calm as she spoke.

Kodiak shook his head a little. He looked worried, so I gave him a reassuring smile.

"We're not accusing him just yet," I said. "There's potential evidence; I don't see the need to throw it away so soon."

*Father's on the line, after all.*

Cody was silent again, then after a long moment of consideration, nodded.

"You're right. I suppose you usually are," he responded with a smirk.

I slightly smiled and blushed modestly. Brushing his comment off, I said, "With our suspect decided on, I say we look for evidence."

"As do I," Lia responded. "Now if we just knew where to start…"

\* \* \*

We had our man. After a good deal of discussion, we decided I would go to the eye doctor's office to search for any possible clues. Meanwhile, Cody and Lydia would be looking for public records elsewhere. Records could take a while to sift through, so having two sets of eyes and hands would help for sure.

I would begin my search the next evening, but while I was currently home, there was something I had been wondering.

Up in my room, carefully holding a precious object in my hands, I sat on my girly, pink bed, gazing intently at the object I held.

I had the music box.

You see, after a while, it had appeared strange to me that when the two lawmen came into our house, one of them had picked up the music box and inspected it. It was a little out of the blue, wasn't it?

*Just what is so interesting about this, anyway?* I wondered. It was pretty, but that wasn't a normal reason for an officer to just pick it up.

I turned it carefully over in my hands.

Nothing seemed particularly suspicious about the object. Maybe I just needed to look more closely?

I inspected its beautiful, gold flower engravings

on the outside; the black plastic on the inside lid; and the little structure in the box's interior, the part that made the music. There wasn't anything unusual.

Turning it upside down again, I examined its surface. It had the initials L.J.L. on it, but I knew that had just stood for Lynette Jade Lothian, as it had been Mother's from when she was a girl. I had her middle name.

After a rather good amount of careful inspection, I couldn't find a thing in the world unusual about the box, so I gave up and put the pretty thing back where it belonged.

"Perhaps," I said aloud to myself, "it is nothing at all, and he was only just a bit curious."

\* \* \*

At the office the next day, I went straight up to Eliza—the lady at the front desk.

She gave me a small smile. "Hello, Felicia. How can I help you?"

"That paper didn't happen to turn up, did it?"

Eliza shook her head sorrowfully.

"I'm afraid not. I'll let you know immediately if I see it."

"Thank you," I replied. I then leaned in close and whispered, "Eliza, do you suppose I could look around behind the front desk?"

She smirked at me. "I can't say I blame you for wanting to. It's fine with me; come on. Look around as much as you'd like, as I'm sure no one will mind."

Opening a drawer, I carefully looked through the papers within, but nothing seemed very important. I opened another and quickly but carefully filed through them. Useless. The third drawer was soon searched, but nothing was worthy of notice. Frustration burned within me, though I concealed it.

There wasn't anything in the whole area that could help.

I let out an aggravated sigh.

"Thank you for letting me look, Eliza."

"Oh, you're welcome. How did it go?"

"I couldn't find anything," I explained. "May I search Father's office again?"

Receiving permission, I then gave two knocks on the office door, opened it up, and saw Miles analyzing a patient's eye exam records on the computer.

"Oh, hi, Felicia. What's up?"

I quickly smiled. "I'm looking for stuff." It felt a bit awkward because I didn't quite know if Mr. Carpenter was to be trusted, though I knew better than to jump to conclusions. There was no need to get too comfortable, though; I needed to retain a healthy caution.

Quietly searching for anything worthy of notice, I subconsciously held my breath, partly due to the desperateness of finding something important and partly due to being a little wary of the intern.

And that was when it happened.

Miles had left for a moment, and as I opened a drawer, I let out a sharp gasp, my blue eyes going wide.

Half concealed was a tight roll of money, tied off with a rubber band. Sure, rolling bills wasn't the traditional way to stack them, but if Miles *was* the person who robbed that house a while back, who was to say he or the victims would have stacked the money traditionally?

Then came another question: Why would Mr. Carpenter have the money stored in my father's office?

From what I could see, the roll was of five-dollar bills. It was all so strange, but soon I heard his footsteps, so I slammed the drawer shut and then stiffly left the office. Inwardly, I was panicking as I passed Miles on the way out, though I tried to remain collected on the outside. In my dread, I unintentionally ignored Eliza's inquiry as to how my search went, thinking only to get out.

\* \* \*

"That's what I saw," I informed Cody and Lia over the home phone at my house. The two were at Lydia's place and sharing the phone as I told them about the money.

"That's insane!" Kodiak somewhat yelled over the line.

"It is crazy, Fay," Lydia added, her voice sounding a bit perplexed. "Certainly mysterious. How did Mr. Carpenter behave?"

"Umm… Pretty calm, actually. He didn't talk much, just examined a patient's eye-exam documents."

"Hmm… Well, make no doubt about it: If he's got money with him, he's definitely a suspect, if for nothing else."

"I'll second that," Cody agreed.

We talked for a little while longer on the subject of the bills, and then I asked, "What did you guys find out while looking through records?"

I could almost *see* Lydia furrowing her eyebrows.

"Actually… nothing."

"What do you mean?"

Cody's voice piped up over the telephone line.

"We searched for *two* hours! But it was all in vain. We looked at records on the locals—past and present—as well as the people in the nearby towns and in Mr. Carpenter's hometown, all that. But we couldn't find a thing in the world about *him*."

"Ugh."

Lydia's voice came on. "I know, right? I'll keep looking."

"Thank you. Keep me posted; I can't really work on further searching tomorrow because I have choir practice after school, and then Mom and I are going to the general store."

Cody lightly laughed over the telephone.

"Sounds fun. All right, if I don't get home soon, *my* Mom's going to be upset; she's probably about done with dinner by now. I'll talk later—and honestly, stay safe. That goes for both of you."

I nodded, even though he couldn't see. "Sure thing, Cody. Thanks."

After saying farewell to them, I hung up.

\* \* \*

Even in the midst of tragedy, life goes on. I certainly learned this during my father's absence. He was gone, but I wasn't. Routine was still the same. There were still all the little tasks that needed to be done.

And so I got up, went to school, left for choir (I was a soprano), finished practice, and then went to the general store with Mother. I couldn't be idle, whether I wanted to or not.

Currently, I was in the canned-goods aisle. Mother was buying pinto beans—lots of them—and I couldn't help but think of Father, for they had always been his favorite type of beans.

Leanne, like any girl, loved coming shopping. I was watching her, as Mom had requested, to make sure she wouldn't wander off or knock anything over. She looked so cute walking around with her ruffly denim dress and big, sandy curls.

Mother went down to another end of the aisle, looking for something else, while Leanne began to go to a different part of the store. I followed her.

"Fay Fay!"

Leanne was one of those little children who never talk much—unlike myself, who had been chattering like a giggling schoolgirl since I was nearly one—so I was a little surprised by her random calling.

"What is it?" I asked softly.

"The coffee!"

She had walked over to the selection of whole-bean coffee bags and was pointing at the type we usually purchase—French roast.

"What about it?" I asked. "We've got enough at home, Leanne."

"It's… Papa's coffee!"

My poor, dear sister. I smiled softly at her.

"Mm-hmm, our father's favorite."

She stared up at me with her big, blue eyes, going back to her usual quietness. Though her voice fell silent, her eyes seemed to be asking me when Father would come home. Only… I couldn't answer.

When I picked her up and was about to walk back to where Mother was, I noticed something, or I suppose I should say *someone,* outside of one of the general-store windows, walking down the sidewalk.

I couldn't pass up this opportunity, even though I was going to feel like a stalker.

Going back to Mom, I said, "Mother, may I go outside?"

"How come, Felicia?"

"It's just really important. May I?"

"Okay, I suppose so. Leanne and I will finish the shopping ourselves."

"Thank you, Mother!"

She briefly smiled, and then I turned and walked quickly out of the store. I felt like running, but that would've seemed suspicious to everyone around me.

Once outside, I walked fairly close to a couple of other citizens, trying to blend in yet all the while keeping my eye on the person across the street, who had caught my attention to begin with.

He looked miserable, all pale and walking stiffly and quickly.

The two other individuals turned into a store, and I was left unblended. Oops.

Where to go? Quickly, I hid behind a side of the building the others had entered.

My eyes turned away from the one I had watched when I saw a dark-red pickup. It slowed down, and the vehicle window on the side further away from me rolled down. I could faintly hear talking but needed to get closer. Uneasily making my way across the street, worrying so much that I'd be noticed, I hid just around the corner from where the interesting sight was taking place. I was hidden, but not at ease.

"It's bad business, Cole. I don't know if coming here was a good idea after all."

"Just tell me what happened, Miles! What's wrong?"

Who was this stranger talking to Mr. Carpenter? And what was such "bad business"?

I could see Miles put a hand to his forehead. "I was so looking forward to your visit, but now you might not even have a place to stay."

*What?*

He cleared his throat, about to continue, when suddenly his phone went off.

"My boss. Go ahead and park, Cole—no need to use your fuel."

Mr. Carpenter answered his phone and started walking as he talked to his boss. He walked away from me, leaving me with no choice but to either follow at a distance or stay where I was. I chose the latter, as I didn't want to take any chances blowing my cover. It was better to play it safe.

Mr. Carpenter walked on for a while, and I wasn't able to hear the conversation. Then, he turned around and started walking toward me again. Soon, he was close enough for me to hear.

"All right, thanks. Talk to you later."

Miles hung up.

*I wonder why his boss called...*

The man in the truck—Cole—having parked, came to where Miles was.

"So," the stranger said, "what's up, then?"

Mr. Carpenter sighed.

Suddenly, and much to my dismay, Mother and Leanne came out of the general store across the street, and I knew my time to leave was near. I lingered for a moment, but when I saw my Mother looking in both directions for me, I knew I'd need to start slipping away. If only I had a minute more!

"Well, it's about Wilsonville," I heard Miles begin.

That stopped me.

"Yes?" Cole inquired.

"I don't know what I'm going to do!" Miles exclaimed, sounding anxious. "I haven't got much money, and *my* house was robbed last night! I don't know *how* I'm going to bring myself to tell Dad and Mom..."

"What?" Cole burst out. "Did you get help?"

I had heard all I strictly needed to hear, though I wanted to know more. Mother called out a "Felicia? Where are you?" and I knew I needed to leave immediately.

Carefully, I slipped away, worried they'd see me but not sure how much it'd matter if they did.

After getting away from the two men, I called, "Right here, Mother!"

"Oh, there you are," she replied, smiling a little. "I was wondering where you had wandered off to and thought maybe it wasn't such a good idea to let you be out alone, with all that's gone on of late."

I nodded, knowing she was referring to there being a robber that had yet to be accounted for.

Deep down, I hid a shudder, because whoever had broken into Mr. Carpenter's house was bad business indeed. He had my father's reputation on the line—and who knew what else?

# THE HOUSE WITH THE WILDFLOWERS

## Chapter 9

So, I clearly had to rule out Miles as the robber because his *own* house had been robbed. After filling Mother in about what the unfortunate intern said, I realized I also needed to inform Cody and Lia immediately. We needed to switch gears—and fast! The criminal, whoever he was, was still at work.

Once I got home, I set right to work. I called Lydia, then Kodiak, and we agreed to meet up at the bus. No time was wasted. I left immediately, after telling Mother, and then biked to the fateful spot.

Cody and Lia were there before too long, their faces full of perplexity and urgency.

After parking her bike, Lia said a bit gloomily, "Well… we've realized we were analyzing the wrong person."

Cody nodded. "Now we need to rethink suspects all over again!"

*If only I could add things up as easily as I can in arithmetic!*

Both of my friends had low spirits, and mine were especially low, but the only way to fix this mess was to put our heads together.

Lydia seemed to recognize that too, as she tuned into her leadership side. "We should inform Uriah."

"Right," I said. "And maybe he'll also know of any other suspects."

In agreement, Cody added, "How about we leave for his place right now?"

Quickly, it was settled, and the three of us biked to Mr. Harper's. It was half-past five o'clock. The sky glowed majestically blue, feathery clouds swirling around in some places, giving off a marbled effect. Birds were twittering, sunshine was all over, and there was a gentle breeze. The atmosphere didn't give off a hint of stress; it was just a typical cheery day for the average person. But I guess we had never been average, anyway.

Arriving, we parked our bikes and went to the front door. Cody rang the doorbell.

Nothing.

Politely, we waited a minute, then two. After still nothing, he rang it again, but we weren't met with any luck.

"Maybe he's not home," the strawberry-blond boy suggested.

"Uriah's truck is still here, though," Lydia replied, pointing toward the driveway.

Something wasn't adding up.

Walking away from the porch, I looked through the windows. The blinds were closed—which was strange, considering the time of day.

"Is that door locked?" I called to my friends.

Cody tested the handle. "Yep."

I walked back over to the two young teens. "I'm going to take a look around the backdoor really quickly," I told them, shuddering upon remembering the events that had previously taken place at Uriah's house.

Lia nodded. "All right. I'm actually going to take a look around the neighborhood, then; I want to check and see if anything is out of place."

Kodiak decided he would stay at the front door and see if anyone would come.

Heading down the sidewalk, Lia carefully observed the houses all lined up. Cody and I watched her for a second, and then I walked to Uriah's backyard.

The wooden fence wasn't locked, which I noticed was strange. Feeling nervous, I opened the gate and peeked through. I ventured into the yard, trying to feel brave. After all, Cody was on the other side of the house—I wasn't completely alone.

There was a gate on the left side of the home as well as on the right. I took the left side on my way in, which revealed most of the backyard. Nothing seemed out of place from what I could see. However, I turned past the corner, leading me to the back porch. The house's blinds were closed, and the windows were broken, of course, from the robbery that had taken place earlier. However, the glass window on the backdoor—which hadn't ever been smashed—revealed, as I cautiously peeked through, that all the lights were turned off except for a small light above the oven.

Heart thumping, I grabbed ahold of the doorknob, and then slowly... so slowly... turned it.

*The door... It isn't even locked!*

I opened it and quietly slipped inside the house. Things were still messed up from the break-in, but I noticed there was a lamp that had been knocked over not far from where I was standing. That hadn't fallen before. And something just seemed... different.

Something was definitely wrong.

I could hear my heart beating, drowning out any other noise. Carefully, I walked toward the kitchen, being mindful not to step on any glass. Uriah had cleaned up all of that before, but you never knew if there could be some very small shards that were missed.

Then I walked into a hallway, which led me to Uriah's personal office. The door was wide open, and the second I entered in, I was frozen in my tracks.

A wall clock ticked mechanically, the only noise. Before me was scattered countless paper shreds— information damaged beyond repair. What had those papers once said? There was no telling now.

I was about to drop to my knees and search through the ruined pieces, when I suddenly heard a thud outside of the room, though I wasn't quite sure where.

I wasn't alone.

Frantically, I spun on my heel and turned out of the hallway. Was Uriah here after all? Or… was it someone else?

Concerned and with a beating heart, I quickly headed toward the backdoor, not wanting to get discovered—but my luck ran out.

In the dim light of the living room, a figure was searching through a drawer on a coffee table. They looked up upon hearing my footsteps.

*Oh no.*

And at that moment, the terrifying figure shouted and winged a book at me.

I dodged it and felt my adrenaline begin to race. For a second, it was as if my thought processes shut down altogether and then had to restart. The angry figure grabbed another book and threw it at me.

I darted away as quickly as possible out the backdoor, gasping for breath as I rushed to the right side of the house. I ran as fast as I could past the rose bushes and through a narrow strip of grass about three feet wide, which led to a gate I had not entered when I came into the backyard earlier. More scared than seems possible, I grabbed the handle and tried to open the gate—only it was locked! I jarred it roughly, inwardly screaming.

"Come on, come on, come on, come on…!"

The horrendous person came running out of the house, and I darted away from the unopenable gate clear to the other side of the backyard, all the while being sure I was doomed.

I hurried out of the other gate just in time.

"Cody!" I shouted. "Watch out!"

The strawberry-blond teen looked toward me, and his jaw dropped. It took him a second to register what was happening, but once he did, he darted off with me, the two of us leaving our bikes behind as we ran in the opposite direction from where we had parked.

My heart was thumping. As my friend and I ran down the sidewalk, we met Lydia, who had been toward the end of the street, finishing up her inspection of the houses. However, it didn't take her more than a second to recognize our impending doom, and she ran off with us.

After a good deal of running, I looked over my shoulder, which I had been afraid to do for a while, and saw that we had outrun the intruder; that person wasn't in sight anymore. I slowed to a stop and panted for breath.

Lia looked from me to Cody with wide eyes. "What happened?"

Briefly motioning behind me, I then looked at Lydia and replied, gasping, "In the house—Uriah's house… I saw—there were—lots and lots of shredded papers, and—then I… Then I saw Mrs. Ennis Norton in there—Will's mother!"

I couldn't believe it! Mrs. Ennis Norton had always been rude, sure—but this? This took "rude" to a whole new level.

Cody shuddered. "She always was cranky, but I never thought she'd resort to breaking into someone's house!"

"Where was Uriah?" Lydia inquired hurriedly, looking at us both intently. "Was he in there?"

My stomach feeling as if it dropped to my toes, I

shook my head. "No, I never saw him."

Kodiak cocked his head to the side. "But his truck was outside?"

Lia shuddered. "The blinds were closed tight."

My friends and I were on to something. If he wasn't home, but his truck was still there, that would seem to imply…

As if reading my mind, Cody burst out, "Has Uriah been kidnapped?"

I couldn't believe it.

Uriah Harper, the stealthy, smart detective, was seemingly captured. I felt anger bubble up inside me.

Unknowingly, I started pacing a little bit, deep in thought. Ennis must have been a very skilled woman to have taken out Uriah.

*We can't do this alone. We're going to need help!*

"Guys," I said, looking at both of my best friends intently. "I know what we need to do. Will Norton can help us. Maybe he can talk Ennis out of this madness."

A spark of determination glimmered in Lydia's eyes. "You're right. But how are we going to get to him? Is it safe to get our bikes back?"

This was where Cody joined in. "Ryker can get us. He's in town right now anyway and has the truck. We can get a ride—come on."

Picking up the pace and running, we knew time

was of the essence. It was only a moment until we saw Ryker and begged to get into the truck.

\* \* \*

"Ennis did *what?*" Ryker yelled, glancing at his younger brother for only a second as we were on the road, holding back his urge to slam on the breaks.

"Chased us out of Uriah's house!" Cody restated.

"And threw a book at me! Two books!" I added, shuddering.

Lia turned her head, looking behind us for any signs of danger. I gazed as well. No one.

*Phew.*

"So yeah, Pitchfork, we gotta get to the Nortons as fast as possible!" Cody exclaimed. "Ennis could be going to their house, and who knows what she may do!"

"Working on it," Ryker replied, not once taking his eyes off the road. He let out a breath slowly. "I hope Dad and Mom aren't going to be upset…"

"There isn't time, though," replied the strawberry-blond boy.

Ryker had a point. I felt a sinking feeling in my stomach. Would *my* father want me to do this? I *needed* to prove him innocent, but—

"Rhys, turn!"

Lydia was looking behind us, and I turned my head in an instant, seeing Ennis in a vehicle not too far away. Having not seen her a minute prior, I knew she must have been speeding quickly. Not good.

One glance in his rearview mirror and Ryker visibly paled like the moon. My heart thumped as he somewhat recklessly turned the steering wheel to the right and, once fully turned, accelerated.

Cody was pushing himself as far back as he could into his seat. "We're going to die, we're going to die, we're going to die…"

"*I'm* going to throw her off our tracks," Ryker said, somewhat to Cody, somewhat to himself. He made another right turn, then another, and then one more to get us back to the spot where we originally saw Ennis. She was no longer on that road anymore, having lost us, and so he drove up straight in the direction of Will and Natasha's.

Lydia gasped in relief. "Oh, Ryker! That was so close. I don't see her anymore."

"Yeah…" he responded. "But I'm worried she's going to report you guys to the police for seeing you at Uriah's house—or at least for seeing Fay there."

Cody turned to Lydia and me, his eyes flashing. "*She* was there first."

Lia nodded. "If I can, I'll call the authorities before she does."

A simple nod from Ryker was given, and then we all grew quiet, praying silently but with our whole hearts that we would get to Will and Natasha's before any more damage could be done.

\* \* \*

Arriving at their house, we seemed to have beat Ennis, for her vehicle was nowhere in sight.

The Norton home looked so peaceful. The sun setting, a pink glow was cast around the sky. The trees were unable to touch the feathery clouds no matter how high they stretched their limbs, and the beautiful wildflowers scattered among the grass gave off a springtime feeling, even if it wasn't.

"Maybe one of us should keep a lookout," Ryker said.

"Good idea," I agreed. "Or maybe even two people."

Ryker and Lia both volunteered, so Cody and I walked up the driveway to the front door. Cody rang the doorbell, and there was a long pause before it opened, revealing Natasha.

"Felicia, Cody, what a surprise! Won't you come in?"

Seeing sweet Natasha in the doorway made my heart sick, considering the news we had to inform her of.

"Oh, Natasha!" I burst out. "I don't know how to say it, but we've made a terrible discovery."

Her eyes widened, and then she exclaimed, "What's the matter?"

Letting us in, she then shut the door and brought us to the living room.

"You guys make yourselves comfortable, please."

We were right about to explain when Owen let out a little cry from another room. Natasha said, "So sorry, I'll be right back; Owen has been very fussy today."

We nodded at her, and she left as we sat down by each other on the cushioned couch.

Whispering to me, Cody said, "How are we supposed to tell her that her mother-in-law's a jerk?"

"I don't know," I whispered back, "but we have to."

A couple of minutes passed, and then Natasha walked in, carrying her baby boy in her arms.

"Will's home. I told him you both were here after I grabbed Owen. I figured you might have also wanted him to hear whatever is troubling you both."

Will had been so busy with his jobs and stuff that I hadn't seen him in a long time. I felt unsettled at the thought of seeing him after all this time only to deliver such painful news.

*His own mother!*

Cody appeared to sense my unease and gave me a slight yet reassuring smile. He didn't know the Nortons as well as my family did, which I imagined only made him feel more awkward.

Rocking Owen gently, Natasha tried to strike up a little small talk, putting us somewhat at ease.

A man of average height walked in, his pale-blue eyes curious. Will Norton took a seat next to his wife and baby boy and then looked at us with a small smile. He looked tired, as I imagined was the fault of his crazy work schedule.

"Hi, guys," he said, running one hand through his black hair. "Sorry to have kept you waiting."

We assured him it was all right, and then we fell silent for a moment, trying to figure out how to break our news to them.

"Well…" I began slowly, "I guess I'm just going to try my best to get right to the point." Blushing, I then gushed out the whole story, with Cody adding in bits here and there.

"She nearly hit Fay with a book, and—"

"A book?" Natasha cut in, stunned.

"A book! In fact, two!"

After every detail was filled in, including the fact that Ennis had sped after us in her car, we fell silent and my heart thumped.

*Oh, what if they don't believe us!*

Will looked over to his wife, his face showing a stunned expression, and then he said slowly, "Why Natasha, these poor children! I… I can't believe this!"

"Is it… really possible?"

"Nat, could you lock the backdoor?"

"Lock your own mother out?" Natasha gasped.

"*If* what Fay and Cody say is true… Mother did always have a temper. But still… I can't imagine she could have done something like… Just lock the door, and we'll think what to do next."

Will fell silent, deep in thought as he stroked his beard.

When Natasha returned from locking the door, Owen stirred in his mother's arms.

Will sighed and put his hand to his head. "I guess you had best get him to sleep. You look tired, Natasha. Why don't you try to rock him in his room for a bit while I sort out this mess?"

"Get me if you need me, please."

She walked out after quickly telling us goodbye.

Natasha had only locked the backdoor, so Will went and locked the front one. "I guess the best thing to do is call the police," he said, seemingly to himself. "Oh, Mother what were you thinking?"

I was about to tell him how Ryker and Lia were still outside, but picking up the phone, he talked over the line, and Cody and I waited, unsure what to do next.

Will was nodding as he talked. "Yes, I understand. Thank you."

Placing the phone back in its place, he turned to us. "Cody? Felicia? Here, I need your help with something."

"But actually—" I began.

"Come on, hurry," Will interrupted.

We followed Mr. Norton to a small hallway on the left side of the living room. There were two doors in the hall, and he opened the one at the end.

"Now," he said, "keep it quiet or I'm going to be upset. Nat's going to have to find out what's going on soon enough."

My heart sank.

"Will?" I questioned. "She's going to find out *what?*"

"I didn't *want* it to come to this, but if I couldn't get that medicine for Owen... I didn't want this to happen, really. If you thought I was just calling the police, though, you're wrong."

I couldn't understand. Cody's face turned like a stone.

"You *monster!*" he gasped.

"Keep it *down!*" Will replied, pushing us into the room and shutting the door.

I heard a key click.

Cody started pounding on the door. "Open up! Open up!"

"Be *quiet!*" Will hissed sharply. "Kodiak!"

Cody stopped pounding for a few seconds. "What did you do? Why are you protecting Ennis Norton?"

"Because she's protecting *me,*" Will replied in a hiss. "I broke into the houses; I was out of work and needed the money for my son. I hated doing it—sure I did—but I couldn't get a fulltime job, and I needed the funds."

My blood ran cold. I grabbed Cody by the shoulders and then motioned to him not to say a word.

I turned to the door.

"Okay, Mr. Norton..." I replied, trying to sound calm. "I know you were worried, but my father is locked up because of—"

"I hate that too, Fay," Will said through the door. "But I knew we could do something to fix that. I've got to go now."

"Wait!" I shouted as I heard him start to walk off. "My family—we *wanted* to help you. Why wouldn't you just let us?"

"I don't take charity. You know that."

We heard the sound of his footsteps leaving. Cody and I were trapped!

Kodiak took a deep breath to steady himself and then turned away from me. "Felicia, a door...!" he said.

Indeed, one was to his left. It had a latch but could be opened from our side. Cody thrust it open, and it revealed a miniature room with an opening—a small entryway, about three feet high, which led to yet another little room made for storage and things. This part was very secluded from the living room and most of the rest of the house.

"Here, Fay, I'll creep in there and see if there's anything important."

I was glad he was going to check. Looking inside from where I stood, I thought it was so dark and spooky, with the stacks of boxes and things in the shadows.

It was only about ten seconds or so until I heard the strawberry-blond boy gasp.

"There's a trapdoor on the floor! I'm going to unlatch it. Hang on—no telling what's down here."

A brief moment passed.

"Got it—hey, there's a ladder."

I heard something faintly, and Cody sucked in his breath.

"Hello?" he called. "Anybody down here?"

"Kodiak?" I asked. "What's going on?"

He didn't answer me, but instead exclaimed, "Uriah!"

My heartbeat accelerated. It was only a moment later that the teen was helping the detective up out of the trapdoor. Uriah's wrists had been tied up, and Cody, pulling out a trusty pocketknife of his, quickly worked on breaking the rope.

"Oh, Uriah!" Cody yelled. "How... long have you been down here?"

"I'm... not sure, to be honest," he replied, his voice hoarse likely from lack of water. "But...it's all

Will—he's the culprit, and his wife doesn't even know. I tried yelling a long time when I was down there," he said, motioning to the room with the trap door. "But after a while I got worn out, and I guess my calls never were heard."

As was the case with pretty much any house, there were windows in our enclosed room. They were medium-sized, and I wasn't sure why Will had put us in a place where we could potentially break open the glass. But then again, we didn't really have anything other than our fists to bust out with. Just in time, though, something—or should I say *someone*—from the window caught my eye.

*Lydia.*

I darted to the window.

"Lia!" I shouted, pounding. "Lia!"

She turned, hearing my plea, and her eyes went wide as her jaw fell open.

Thumping her palms onto the window, she yelled, "Fay!"

Cody was by my side at an instant, followed by Uriah.

Looking at my best friend through the glass, I yelled, "It's Will Norton! He's done it all!"

Lydia turned pale but nodded sharply. "Okay, hang on! I'm going to distract them—we'll get you guys out!"

She ran off, and I peered through the window.

*Will Norton of all people!*

Tearing myself away from the spot, I turned toward Cody and Mr. Harper. There was nothing to say, so I just carefully surveyed the room. If only there were an opening! Maybe Uriah could kick the glass…

There wasn't a need. In an instant, something else was being bust open instead. The door that enclosed us fell with a thud, and I held back a scream. But we were met with the anxious face of Ryker Nobleman, seized with adrenaline, who shouted for us to "Make a mad dash and run for it!"

We did just that.

Darting out of the room, the three of us fled from our imprisonment, running after Ryker and also Lydia. The front door was wide open. Natasha appeared in the hallway, having left her son in his cradle. She was stunned, unaware of why there was such a commotion.

"Will!"

The said person appeared at the doorway, just as we were about to run through, and Uriah—somehow summoning within himself strength, despite his exhaustion and dehydration—shoved Will into the wall.

"Mr. Norton…" he said, panting. "You ought to be ashamed of yourself!"

# Conquerors

## Chapter 10

Was it really true, or was I dreaming? Father was released!

But Will and Ennis Norton—my heart ached for Natasha and Owen. Natasha would have to raise her son on her own for a time.

At the Furnas County Sheriff's office, my heart skipped a beat as my dad was freed.

"Father!" I shouted, unable to contain myself while running toward him.

"My Funnel Cake!"

I crushed him in a warm hug, not wanting to let go. He was really back! Free!

Feeling so happy I could burst, I practically skipped as the four of us walked outside.

"Well now," Father began with a smile, "shall we go to the park? The weather seems to be perfect today."

"Could we?" I exclaimed.

Mother laughed. "I don't see why not."

The plan was to go to Cody's house later that day, but we had several hours before that to spend time together as a family.

Hopping into the truck, it didn't take long at all for us to arrive at the park. Father and Mother walked around, looking at the changing leaves, while I took Leanne to the swings and such.

"Now hold onto the chains," I said, helping her up onto a swing that was low to the ground. Her little hands gripped on tight.

Smiling, I pushed her, and she giggled in delight.

"Fay Fay! Higher, higher!"

"Okay," I said, grinning. "Hold on tighter!"

A gentle breeze blew, tossing my curls behind me, and I tilted my face toward the sun. Everything was perfect again. We were a happy family. My eyes wandered to the sight of my cheery parents walking together, and then back to my laughing little sister. The struggles had finally ceased. Father's name was cleared.

A sparrow, landing on a branch nearby, twittered. It seemed to be singing a song as blissful as my heart felt. In a way, I longed to sing with it. I did have that choir event coming up, after all...

As I reflected on the past events of my life, something resurfaced in my mind.

Pushing Leanne for a bit longer, I sighed and then, with a smile, slowly brought the swing to a stop. "Come on, Leanne, let's go see Father and Mother."

I grabbed her tiny hand, and the two of us walked through the grass toward our parents. They smiled at her and me, and I fell into step with them as Father picked up Leanne.

We were silent for a little while, looking at the things around us, and then Leanne started to talk to Father with her small sentences. I turned to my mom.

"Mother..." I began.

"Yes, Fay?"

"You know when those lawmen came to the house, when they... took Father? Well, for a second... I thought that since we have Dad back, everything is solved—no more mystery. But now I remember there's one thing that confuses me still."

"Really? What is it?"

"When the men were searching the house, one of them seemed a bit interested in my music box. He inspected it out of the blue, and I never understood why; it didn't seem to have anything to do with a robber. I know it's kind of weird for me to care about it, and maybe he was simply curious, but... I still wonder sometimes."

Mother smiled softly. "Hmm, is that so? I think I

may know why the lawman did what he did."

My eyes widened. "Really? Why?"

"You remember that it used to be mine, correct?"

"Yes."

"Well, when I was a girl, I used to have two music boxes, but one of them was stolen when I was a teenager. It had been a very special sweet-sixteen gift from my American grandparents, and I was quite upset. I've never seen it since, but when Reece saw how heartbroken I was, it made him hate stealing with a passion—he saw how much it hurt people. Back when it was taken, I had reported to the authorities that it went missing, and that lawman you met is the same one I reported it to as a teenager. I still remember that day. He is rather old now—I should think he'd be getting close to retirement—but it makes me wonder if he saw your music box and thought it may have been the one I lost. I imagine he recognized it didn't fit the description after a moment."

"Wow, Mother," I breathed. After a moment of reflecting on the subject, I said, "Do you think you'll ever see your old one again?"

She smiled. "I don't know. Probably not, but I guess I've moved on. If I could ever recover it, though, I'd be awfully glad."

"Me too," I said. The singing of the sparrow came to my attention again, and I listened thoughtfully to its sweet song.

"I think… that one day, maybe one day, you'll

find it, Mother."

* * *

Later when we got home, I was with Father in his office. He was showing me stuff about the stock market, something that I always found interesting. The little colored lines zigzagged across the screen, some rising, others falling. I gazed at these things called candlesticks, showing the high and low prices for each day.

"I hadn't been able to do anything with my stocks while I was away," Father explained. "Looks like I missed some pretty interesting stuff. I would have enjoyed selling some stock here, see?"

I looked at the day he pointed to and nodded. One stock in particular was selling for a lot of money then. Today, the stocks for that same company were selling cheap, so he didn't need to get rid of any from that section. However, another company was selling high, and he had a few good stocks he didn't mind selling from it.

"I don't like spending too long looking at it all," Father informed. "I'm busy enough as is, personally, but I don't mind having some stocks and investing a little here and there."

It seemed like a good idea. Father did well at managing his time.

There were lots of little numbers on the charts, some good, some not so good.

Statistics were fascinating! I eyed some more stock-market candlesticks. Breathing in the smell of the office's *actual* candle, which was apple pie scented, I sighed contently. One thing was certain: I would never take for granted my time with Father, in his office or anywhere. When he was gone, there were so many times I would have given whatever I had just to sit by him at his desk or be with him outside on the porch swing, chatting or learning.

Savoring these moments, I pulled up a comfortable chair and discussed the stock market.

\* \* \*

That evening, we arrived at Cody's house, as was planned. The adults were chatting in the kitchen while Ryker, Kodiak, Lydia, and I were standing in the living room.

"As soon as I told Rhys about how you guys were locked in the room at the Nortons', we darted to the front door," Lydia explained. "It was bolted, so Ryker knocked firmly, and as soon as Will opened the door, he shoved Mr. Norton out of the way and ran to the room you guys were in. Granted, we didn't really know the layout of the house that well, but we managed."

"Yeah," Ryker agreed. "Something felt off once we got there, I thought, but I couldn't place it. Everything seemed even more suspicious once it took you both a long while to come out, though."

"It was scary," I replied with a slight shudder. "What a beginning to teenhood this has been— having my father taken away *and* getting kidnapped by a robber!"

Cody gave me an encouraging look and said, "But we made it. *You* made it."

*I guess I did, didn't I?*

He gave me a high five, fitting his personality, and just after, the doorbell rang.

Ryker went to answer, and as the door opened, I heard him call, "Hello, Mr. Carpenter! And Mr. Harper! Glad you guys could join us."

The Noblemans had invited Miles and Uriah over, as well as all of us, which was typical of their kind hospitality.

"We've got the whole gang here," Cody said with a laugh. He went to fist bump Uriah and then carried on a conversation with Miles.

I blushed a little, remembering our past suspicions. Lia and I exchanged glances, and then we went to greet the guests.

My heart felt full with everyone gathered together in the Nobleman home. I was motionless, taking in the view of colored leaves falling from the trees through the windows, smelling the aroma of freshly baked snickerdoodles in the kitchen, and hearing the sound of chatter and laughter by those I held dear. For a moment, it was as if time paused. I breathed in deeply and then slowly let out a contented sigh. Father held Leanne, who seemed to never want to let him go, and Mother checked a pan of cauliflower while Mrs. Nobleman took a bowl of coleslaw out of the fridge.

Lydia's grandmother was washing pans as all the

men went outside to the porch, taking in the wonders of nature. (The women insisted that the men relax, you see.)

Meanwhile, in the kitchen, the ladies chattered and laughed. I smiled to myself as I heard Mother explain how she made her "spicy potato salad." We had brought some today, considering that all the men, especially my father, loved its extra kick. Personally, I enjoyed it too; cayenne pepper is amazing!

Plopping onto the couch, I inhaled and closed my eyes.

Kodiak thumped down next to me on the left side of the couch, and Lydia thumped down on my right. Cody had "snuck" some snickerdoodles and gave one each to Lia and me, keeping one (or two) for himself as well, of course.

Accepting the cookie, Lia then turned to me. "This past month or so sure has been an adventure... Life's a crazy thing—great, though... crazy still."

Cody looked at us both, a slight smirk covering his face. "Well after all, if life were easy, it wouldn't have meaning."

Slightly laughing, Lia pondered Cody's remark and replied, "Wow, Cody, that was actually deep."

We joked for a bit despite our past troubles and then fell silent. As I looked at my two friends, a thought crossed my mind.

"You know what, guys?"

"What?"

"I would have never made it if it wasn't for you both."

Lydia beamed. "We're friends—best friends, each of us. Friends help each other up when they fall into a tricky situation. I know you guys have been there for me again and again."

"Same here," Cody agreed. "We all need each other and help each other."

They were right. True friends were the ones who were there. They always listened to you when you needed them to, could help when you were hurting by simply being near, and just made life a little sweeter overall.

That was exactly what Cody and Lia did.

"Guys," Lydia began, "I don't know what we're going to face next, but I know we can endure it. It may not be easy, and I don't expect it to be, but... I'm going to do my best to enjoy every day I have. We can withstand the storms."

What adventures and troubles lay ahead? There was no telling—but as Lia said, we would be okay. I knew we would.

I flashed my friends a smile.

## ABOUT THE AUTHOR

DANIELLE RENEE WALLACE is a teenage author born in Washington State. She established a large love for reading during her elementary school years and a strong love for writing while in middle school. At fourteen, Danielle published her first book, while living in Lubbock, Texas. Her father spent about one year of his boyhood in Wilsonville, Nebraska, the town in which Danielle's series, *Secrets of the Abandoned Bus,* takes place. Currently, she resides in northern Ohio with her parents and two older brothers.

Made in the USA
Monee, IL
21 May 2022